"I can't tell if it's Sophie and my ex-husband from this picture."

Garnet continued to explain, "It's too far away and fuzzy. If the man is my ex, he's had a makeover. Yet this girl's smile is so like Sophie's my chest aches to see it. I'd give anything just to hug her again."

Without warning, Garnet burst into tears and the snapshot fell to the floor.

Unable to stand by while she fell apart, Julian did what came naturally. He wrapped Garnet in a tight embrace. Feeling her stiffen, he immediately let go. However, her tears didn't stop.

Saying a silent *to hell with it,* Julian moved in again, and held her until her tears were spent.

Dear Reader,

The most asked question of an author is "Where do your ideas come from?" The answer is as diverse as the stories themselves. For me it's usually a snippet I read about or overhear that nags me to write my own version, as it was in this case.

A few years ago a reader wrote to say she'd read one of my books. In the letter she mentioned truth being stranger than fiction. Her husband, she said, a postman, was instrumental in reconnecting a child—pictured on one of the lost-children cards he delivered—with the child's mother. Off and on I found myself wondering how it has all worked out. But since I didn't know the "real" story, I made up how I'd like such a reunion to turn out. I like happy endings, and I like good people. I took liberties with this story that probably aren't true to life. Especially as I have a friend in social work who says domestic abductions rarely end well. More often than not the child ends up hurt, because children love both mom and dad equally.

In this book I wanted to delve into the feelings and emotions of two parents involved in such a case. And since it's fiction, I really wanted the best possible ending for my stolen child, Sophie Patton. I hope you like her story.

Roz Denny Fox

P.S. Readers can contact me at P.O. Box 17480-101, Tucson, AZ 85731 or rdfox@worldnet.att.net.

LOOKING FOR SOPHIE
Roz Denny Fox

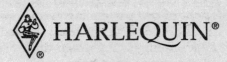

HARLEQUIN®

TORONTO • NEW YORK • LONDON
AMSTERDAM • PARIS • SYDNEY • HAMBURG
STOCKHOLM • ATHENS • TOKYO • MILAN • MADRID
PRAGUE • WARSAW • BUDAPEST • AUCKLAND

ISBN-13: 978-0-373-71459-9
ISBN-10:   0-373-71459-9

LOOKING FOR SOPHIE

www.eHarlequin.com

Printed in U.S.A.

ABOUT THE AUTHOR

Roz Denny Fox has been a RITA® Award finalist and has placed in a number of other contests; her books have also appeared on the Waldenbooks bestseller list. Roz currently resides in Tucson, Arizona, with her husband, Denny. They have two daughters.

Books by Roz Denny Fox

HARLEQUIN SUPERROMANCE

1069–THE SEVEN YEAR SECRET
1108–SOMEONE TO WATCH OVER ME
1128–THE SECRET DAUGHTER
1148–MARRIED IN HASTE
1184–A COWBOY AT HEART
1220–DADDY'S LITTLE MATCHMAKER
1254–SHE WALKS THE LINE
1290–A MOM FOR MATTHEW
1320–MORE TO TEXAS THAN COWBOYS
1368–ANGELS OF THE BIG SKY
1388–ON ANGEL WINGS
1412–REAL COWBOYS

HARLEQUIN EVERLASTING LOVE

13–A SECRET TO TELL YOU

HARLEQUIN AMERICAN ROMANCE

1036–TOO MANY BROTHERS
1087–THE SECRET WEDDING DRESS

HARLEQUIN SIGNATURE SAGA

COFFEE IN THE MORNING
HOT CHOCOLATE ON A COLD DAY

CHAPTER ONE

JULIAN CAVENAUGH closed the folder and pushed his chair back from his desk. He and his partner, Rick Barnett, had finally cracked the case after four months of tracking leads, many of which had gone nowhere, leaving everyone frustrated. Even as a veteran detective in one of Atlanta's grittiest precincts, he felt good about putting another alleged murderer behind bars. His chief had suggested he take a vacation now before plunging into his next case. Rick had already taken his family to Florida for sun and fun. But Julian hadn't decided yet. Too much downtime could make him lose his edge.

He was, however, toying with the idea of going fishing with his dad for a couple of days. Even though his family lived just thirty miles outside Atlanta, Julian hadn't seen them since Christmas. His crazy schedule hadn't allowed it.

His phone rang, jerking him back to attention. "Cavenaugh," he snapped.

"Julian, it's Mom."

He gripped the receiver tighter, thinking maybe he'd conjured up this call. "What's wrong?" Neglectful or not, Julian couldn't remember his family ever phoning him at the office. They left messages at his apartment or on his cell because no one wanted to bother him at work.

"It's your dad." Beth Cavenaugh's voice sounded odd.

"Is it his heart? How bad? Damn, we all warned him at Christmas to lay off the rich desserts." Julian glanced at the wall clock. "If I leave now, I can be in Mosswood in under an hour."

"I'm sorry, I don't mean to frighten you. Your father is well enough." Beth lowered her voice. "He's done it again, Julian. Sam is positive he's recognized one of the kids on his route from a card. Oh, I shouldn't bother you. I did try Taggert and Josh first, but they refuse to talk to him. And he's not listening to me. I've reminded him he's only got six months until he can retire and the department will drop the earlier reprimand so he goes out with a clean record, but Sam claims this isn't about him. And…Julian…what if he's right this time?"

Shutting his eyes, Julian rubbed the back of his neck. "Listen, I just closed a big case—the west-end serial murders. You've probably seen it on the news. Chief MacHale wants me to take some time off. Let me tie up some loose ends here, then I'll come down to see you tomorrow. Maybe I can reason with Pop."

"Oh, would you? I didn't want to ask, but this is so much like the last time. He's a stubborn old coot when he gets it in his head that he's right. It's not like he's even seen this little girl up close. They're a fairly new family on his mail route. I just want him to be careful and not make wild accusations again."

Julian tried to reassure his mother. "Don't worry. I have avenues to check that we didn't have before."

Beth seemed relieved and before hanging up they arranged that he'd arrive around one the next day.

Julian sat quietly for a moment, letting his thoughts drift back to the disaster that had his mother concerned even now. He'd been a high-school sophomore. Tag and Josh were in junior high and Celeste still in grade school. Tag had invited a new friend home for supper. After the boy left the Cavenaughs, Sam had pulled out a card sent by the National Center for Missing and Exploited Children. Sam delivered one or two of the cards along his route every week, and he kept copies for himself. The whole family had agreed the new boy was a dead ringer for a kid listed as missing from a nearby state.

But within hours of Sam calling the hotline all hell broke loose in sleepy Mosswood. An FBI team swept in and the scandal that followed their investigation was huge. Bigger than huge. Tag's friend *wasn't* the missing boy. And rather than praising Sam Cavenaugh for doing his civic duty, the boy's dad, rich as Warren Buffett, did his best to get Sam fired. Mr. Miller was so angry over the scrutiny and suspicion he and his family were forced to endure, he closed a factory he'd recently opened in town. A hundred residents lost their jobs.

For a while, the Cavenaughs were pariahs. If the NCMEC hadn't supported Samuel, he would've been fired. The agency spokesman released a statement asking where lost and stolen kids would be if people like Sam Cavenaugh never stuck their necks out? All the same, an official reprimand went on Sam's record. It took years for the town to forgive and forget.

Julian knew that his father had done the right thing. All cops relied on citizen tips in their cases. Still, Julian understood why his mom was worried.

Julian quickly exited his shared office and left his file on the murder case in the clerk's out-basket where Rick Barnett had already left his. Down the hall, he knocked on Chief MacHale's door.

"I don't want to see you for at least two weeks," Conrad MacHale said, signing and dating the vacation request Julian handed him. "No two or three days and you're back." MacHale paused to examine him more closely. "Man, you look like hell—like you haven't slept since this case started. Go relax. Get on that motorcycle you're so fond of, find a hot date and have a good time. Just don't come back for two weeks. A month would be better, but we can't spare you that long."

"In a month a guy could forget how to do the job."

"I doubt that." MacHale's laugh was dry as he passed Julian a copy of the form. "Your record's one of the best in the precinct, if not the whole town."

Julian left the chief's office smiling, but without responding to the rare compliment. Mac didn't give them often and he wouldn't appreciate gushy thanks. All the same, his comment went a long way toward relieving Julian's fatigue. And he was tired. This last case had taken a long four months.

Still, there was no job he'd rather have. A collar

like the one he'd just made made up for all the crappy days. Their team had solid DNA evidence linking Fred Struthers to a string of rapes and murders in a normally secure section of town. With Struthers in custody, residents and cops could breathe easier.

As he left the building, heading home, Julian remembered his folks hadn't been overjoyed with his career choice. They both had safe jobs, as they pointed out. Sam had delivered mail for almost thirty years come rain, snow or blistering sun. Beth sold real estate part-time. Their combined income left them comfortably middle-class, and had made it possible for their four kids to attend university. At thirty-one, Tag managed a swank Atlanta hotel. Josh, twenty-nine, was a news anchor at the local TV station. Celeste, the baby at twenty-eight, worked as a neonatal nurse now that her twin girls had started school.

Julian's siblings were all happily married and had given his folks grandbabies to spoil. He would've thought they'd be happy with that. But any time he made it to Mosswood for family gatherings, he felt subtle—if not overt—pressure, to get married. One Cavenaugh or another would invite an unsuspecting single woman to dinner for the express purpose of shoving her at Julian.

Celeste, married to a doctor, had once asked if he ever met women at work. He grinned to himself, recalling her face when he'd said, "Sure, sis. Hookers." That had effectively put an end to questions for that meal. Of course, he knew Celeste was asking if he met any nice single women cops. Cops marrying cops worked for some, but Julian preferred not to talk shop 24/7. When he got home, he wanted to leave the world's troubles behind. His time off was erratic, which made regular dating difficult. It was a big reason why, at thirty-three, he was still unmarried and okay with it. Mostly. At times, he envied his siblings….

THE NEXT DAY, after packing the saddle bags on his custom black-and-chrome Ducati Monster, Julian cruised the back roads to Mosswood. He loved feeling the wind in his face. Spring in Georgia could be muggy or mild; today was pleasant. Sunshine filtered through a canopy of hickory and sweet-gum trees, late-blooming dogwoods still had enough waxy blossoms to entice photography buffs out of their cars.

The scent of honeysuckle permeated the air, and Julian glimpsed a pair of yellow-throated warblers flitting among the bushes. He'd forgotten how freedom felt.

He didn't bother planning how to approach his dad. Sam Cavenaugh's love for his kids wasn't complicated. Julian knew they'd be able to talk openly and honestly about what was worrying Beth.

Julian motored along his parents' tree-lined street. His family's redbrick home complemented a backdrop of well-tended flowerbeds and a manicured lawn. Julian and his siblings had grown up here, and the sight of the house always made him nostalgic. Of the four Cavenaugh kids, Julian was least likely to ever need a five-bedroom home. Still at every get-together, he said, "Remember, if you two ever want to downsize, I'd be happy to take it off your hands."

His mom must have been watching for him. Julian had barely parked his bike in the drive and removed his helmet when she burst from the house, ran to meet him and engulfed him in a hug. Like all her boys, Julian towered over Beth's petite five-two frame. Because she loved to cook, she tended to be on the plump side. The fact Julian looked gaunt didn't escape her eagle eye.

"Sakes alive, I can see there's no doughnut shop near your station. Well, no matter, I'm fixing your favorite meal tonight. No objections, now," she said when Julian opened his mouth. "And I've invited a nice young woman to join us. A new member of my gourmet cooking club. Such a sweet girl. I just know you're going to love her."

"Ma, I came because you asked me to talk to Pop. If this visit is really about you matchmaking, I'm getting right back on my bike."

His mother kept a firm hold on his arm as she steered him inside. "Honestly, I thought you prided yourself on juggling a dozen cases at once. Are you saying you can't meet a pretty girl *and* head your dad off at the pass?"

"I'm saying I'm not looking for a wife. If that's why you invited the gourmet cook to join us for dinner, uninvite her. Besides, the fewer people who hear about Pop's sighting another missing child, the better."

"You're right." Beth pouted a bit as they entered the house, but she picked up the phone anyway, so Julian knew he'd made his point.

He'd unpacked a few shirts and was seated at the kitchen table enjoying a cold beer, when his dad ambled in from work. Sam greeted his son with a slap on his back that morphed into a sort of hug.

"Hey, stranger. I hear you caught the guy you were looking for. Congratulations! I assume that's why Mom and I have the pleasure of your company. Good work, son."

"Thanks. It was a tough case. The chief wants me rested and ready to testify at the trial. I thought I'd see if you felt like tossing a line in the river. Why don't you grab a beer? We can go sit on the back porch and discuss the best fishing hole."

"Sorry, son. You'll have to go fishing alone. I'm involved in a bit of surveillance, myself."

"Oh?" Julian feigned surprise.

"Let me get that beer. And then we'll go out where your mom can't overhear us. She thinks I'm a meddling old fool but I know I'm right this time. Actually, I'm glad you're here. This is right up your alley."

Julian had thought he'd have to pump his dad for information. This was almost too easy, he decided, twisting the cap off a second bottle of light beer.

Once they'd settled into matching wicker rockers, Sam leaned toward Julian and began his story. "There's this new family on my postal route, see. They moved in about four months ago. A mom, dad and three kids. Two boys go to school and, like normal kids, are out tossing a ball or riding bikes when they get home. The girl, a pretty little tyke, looks out the window until someone inside notices and closes the drapes. I call that odd. Something's not right. So, I go to my file of missing-children cards and bingo, I see a kid that could be her, only younger. Same hair, same heart-shaped face. If you were me, wouldn't you call the hotline?"

Julian took a swig from his bottle and rocked back in his chair. "I might remember the last time this happened and take it kinda easy, Pop."

"Yeah, yeah. That other time was unfortunate. I missed a big clue. That boy was out around town, attending school. I'm smarter now. I'm keeping an eye on this family."

Julian picked at the label on his beer. "You see any evidence this girl's being abused?"

"No. But, shouldn't a five- or six-year-old be in school, or out playing with her brothers? If they *are* her brothers. She's blond as blond can be. The boys are dark eyed and dark haired. Dad's got long black hair. He ties it back like some young fellas do. I've only seen the mother once. She has sorta nut-brown hair."

"The man, does he act sneaky or is he a tough-guy sort?"

"Uh, he's not real neighborly. Grunts hello if I'm putting mail in his box when he arrives home from work. He's blue-collar. He always wears jeans and a work shirt and they're often greasy. A couple of Saturdays I've seen him in the driveway shooting hoops with the boys. And they barbecue out back."

"Sounds like a normal family. He play with all three kids?"

"Their fence is six feet high. I'm not about to give myself away by peeking over it. I'm telling you, Julian. My gut tells me something's fishy."

"You're real close to retirement, Pop."

"Now you sound like your mom. You think I should turn a blind eye?"

Julian fidgeted. His dad clearly felt the girl didn't belong to that family. While he'd come here to help his mother talk his dad out of doing something foolish, Julian understood gut feelings. Sometimes acting on them broke a case. Even knowing that his mom wouldn't appreciate it, he couldn't help saying, "I could fill in for you on your route the next couple of days. See what I observe. I still have the relief-worker status I got that time you wrecked your back."

"That's an idea. I'll pick up the mail from the station and tell my boss that I hurt my knee but you're home and can help out. He'll jump on that. He hates the hassle of requesting a relief person."

"I remember that. I'd rather go fishing, but surveillance is my forte." Julian didn't add that if he could prove that Sam was definitely wrong, Beth could stop worrying.

Rather than take Sam's postal cart the next day, Julian loaded mail in his bike saddlebags. He took his cell phone along so he could snap pictures from a safe distance. Before heading off, he studied the card with the photo of the missing girl. It was a grainy black-and-white shot. "Pop, this kid was last seen in Anchorage, Alaska, over a year ago. It's a stretch to think she'd wind up in backwater Georgia. Another thing, don't kids this age change a lot in a year? I'm thinking of Celeste's twins. I see them occasionally, but at each visit they look so different I don't know which twin is which."

"Their smiles and face shape don't change."

Julian had to give give his dad that. He started the Ducati and drove off. Most old-timers on the route knew him and many expressed concern for Sam. Julian stuck to the story about his dad's bum knee.

His father had told him which house to watch for, so when he got there, Julian took his sweet time sorting out the mail. A few bills addressed to Lee Hackett, some junk circulars. Julian had timed his delivery to coincide with school dismissal. Sure enough, two grade-school-aged boys stopped to admire his motorcycle. Introducing himself, Julian handed them the mail while casually asking their names.

"I'm Toby, he's Gavin," the youngest said. "Our dad used to have a blue Harley," he volunteered.

"Cool. Did he sell it?" Julian asked, gazing into the open, empty garage attached to the side of a small house that sat back off the street.

"I meant our *real* dad. He died. Uh, maybe Lee had a bike, too. I bet he fixes them. Lee's a mechanic."

"Ah…so, Mr. Hackett's your stepfather?" Julian tucked the rest of the mail back into the saddlebag.

Toby hesitated before saying, "Lee wants to adopt me and Gavin. Mom said it takes money, though. More money than we've got."

The older boy grabbed his brother's arm and pulled him up the drive. "Where's the old dude who usually brings our mail?" He eyed Julian suspiciously.

"My dad wrenched his knee. The doc wants him to stay off it a couple of days. When I was your age I helped with his route. I'm down from Atlanta on vacation."

A woman stuck her head out a door opening into the garage. "You boys get inside and change out of your school clothes. Who are you talking to?"

"The mailman's son," the eldest boy shouted.

Julian glimpsed a curly-haired girl poking her head out around her mother's leg. The boys' backs were turned, so he opened his cell and snapped two photos. By the time the youngest boy turned back, Julian had punched in Josh's number and wandered back to his bike with the phone at his ear. Toby waved nonchalantly before he and his brother ran into the house.

Josh picked up as Julian casually straddled his bike, giving the appearance of being in no rush to leave. "Hey, son of a gun, I wangled a few days off. I'm staying with the folks, but Mom's up to her usual tricks. Last night I talked her out of inviting a woman to dinner. Tonight I need an excuse to escape. You and Dawn going to be home later?"

Josh sounded delighted, so the brothers made plans to get together. Julian was stowing his phone when he noticed the girl peering out between the front drapes. He got off two more quick shots before one of her brothers yanked her out of sight and their mother appeared. She stared at Julian, then adjusted the panels. He definitely got the feeling that she didn't want him hanging around.

He wheeled his bike down the street to the next mailbox, stopping where the woman could see him if she chose to look. And Julian thought maybe she did, so he took his time delivering the mail and making chitchat with neighbors.

He made a point of passing back by the Hackett house on his way home. Luck was with him. A man was pulling into the garage as Julian motored past. He noted the license number on the unremarkable minivan.

The minute he reached his parents' home, he logged on to a secure Web site and ran the plate through the state system. It checked out okay. The van was licensed to Lee Hackett at that street address. A separate probe didn't turn up any prior convictions or outstanding warrants for Hackett in Georgia. For kicks, Julian tried Alaska. Nothing showed up there, either.

He found his dad out back weeding. "Pop, can you take another day off? I'd like to do your route in reverse so I hit Hackett's about the time he gets home from work. One of his sons told me he probably fixes motorcycles. I might be able to start a conversation. So far, though, they seem fine. One of the neighbors told me the girl, Leah, has asthma. That could explain her staying indoors. Or maybe the parents are worried about stranger abductions. Some folks are these days. Or couldn't they just be antisocial?"

"I suppose." Sam removed his gardening gloves and walked back to the house with his son. Julian handed back the missing-children card. "Thanks for digging in, son, and for finding out Hackett's not wanted by the law."

"No problem. I put out discreet feelers on the mom of the missing girl through a P.I. contact who can access background info on anyone. That report will take a day or so, provided she hasn't left Alaska. By the way, I'm having dinner with Josh and Dawn tonight. Will you tell Mom? And remind her she doesn't need to set me up with the woman from her cooking club tomorrow night, either."

Sam gave a robust laugh. "I told Beth that gal doesn't have enough spunk for you, son. But your mom's not gonna rest until you've found a wife."

"Then she won't rest for a long time."

His dad's laughter was slow to die. "What's that mean? You saying you've been in one of those closets?"

That was about the last remark Julian expected from his dad, and it took him aback. Finally, he was able to laugh. "No, Pop. I like women just fine. I'm picky, that's all. I'm holding out for someone like Mom."

"That'll take a lot of looking. Your mother is one in a million. Oh, I know she gets upset with me. But she's a peach. And I'm a damn lucky man."

"Yep, but Mom's worried you're mistaken about the Hackett girl. Another reprimand could lose you your pension. Is that the way to repay Mom's love and loyalty?"

"Well, now. Why not just come right out and call me a doddering buttinsky?"

"It's not that, Pop. I want you to think about the risks and proceed with caution."

"I am. I haven't called the FBI or the missing kids hotline."

"Good. I've got two weeks off. My time is yours on this. The girl on the card, Sophie Patton…she's been missing over a year. Trails go cold. Just…don't get antsy."

"As long as they don't look like they're packing up. School's out soon. The NCMEC folks told me last time that people running with stolen kids don't usually stay in one spot longer than a school year. I asked Hackett once why his daughter wasn't in school with her brothers. He said at least three times in the space of a minute that she's only four. She looks older to me."

"When's school out?"

"Two weeks."

THE NEXT DAY Julian felt even more pressure to turn up something useful on Lee Hackett. Both of his brothers and their wives had expressed their concern about his father's meddling at dinner the previous evening. Tag and Raine had declared Sam was nuts. Josh and Dawn asked Julian to put a stop to what they were sure spelled disaster. And the four of them were dead certain he was way off base.

Julian ended his deliveries at the Hacketts'. They had a package with their bundle of mail, a box addressed to Toby Roberts. The return address was a Mrs. Leland Carter of Macks Creek, Missouri. Toby, Julian recalled, had been friendly, the boy who said Lee Hackett wasn't his and Gavin's real dad.

Julian could've squished the package into the mailbox, but decided to take the opportunity to knock on the door. This afternoon it was evident there were children playing in the backyard. Julian heard a ball bounce on cement. He rang the doorbell and caught a glimpse of the blond girl as she swept back the curtain, then scampered out of sight.

A few seconds passed. Suddenly Gavin opened the door. He snatched the package and slammed the door in Julian's face just as Lee Hackett turned in to the driveway. The man parked in the garage, leaped from his van and eyed Julian warily. "Whatcha want?"

"Just delivering a package that was too big for your mailbox." Julian walked down the steps, repeating the lie about his dad's twisted knee.

Hackett's dark eyes flashed to Julian's bike. "Great Ducati Monster," he exclaimed.

Happy his strategy was working, Julian rattled off its stats. Hackett followed Julian to the street and knelt beside the bike, running a work-worn hand over the chrome exhaust. The man knew his motorcycles, Julian decided by the time Hackett excused himself to return to his house.

Julian was fastening his helmet strap when the

side door of the house flew open and the blond girl launched herself into Hackett's arms. Caught off guard, Julian fumbled for his phone. He managed to snap a few shots, hoping that at least one would be good. He took one last picture as Hackett picked up the girl and swung her up and around like an airplane. Hackett grinned at his daughter and tossed Julian a quick wave before going into the house. He looked like any dad happy to be home with his kids after a hard day's work.

Julian could barely contain his excitement as he rode to his folks' house to download his pictures. When he finally made it, Julian wanted to rip them out of the printer. "Pop, come here," he called, setting the first photo on the desk. "Does this girl look like she's being held against her will?" There was pure joy in the child's wide smile and in the way she clasped her dad's face between her hands.

Sam came in from the living room, and had to agree with his son's assessment. "Yeah. But wouldn't that be the case if he's a noncustodial parent? And it doesn't make him less guilty of a crime. Son, I swear I'd rip this card up if I could be sure that girl isn't Sophie Patton. Imagine if you were her mom. Hell, what if your mother and I had divorced and the court gave you to her, but I waltzed in and whisked you away? Wouldn't she be sick about it?"

Julian slid the pictures into a file folder he'd started on Hackett. "Mom would go after you with a shotgun." They shared a chuckle before Julian sobered. "My inquiry on Sophie's custodial parent came in from Doug, my P.I. contact. Her mother, Garnet, teaches English at an Anchorage high school. Has for more than five years."

"Doesn't prove anything. Maybe she can't afford to chase after her girl."

"Hmm. You know, I met a cop from Anchorage a few years back at a domestic violence seminar. Larry Adams. We hit it off, 'cause we're both outdoor types. He said Alaska has great fishing. Maybe I'll phone him…see what he can tell me about the old case."

Beth Cavenaugh walked in on the men and heard her son's last comment. "Won't another police officer wonder why you're asking questions, Julian? Perhaps you ought to fly up there to fish, and poke around by yourself."

"It's way out of my jurisdiction. But I'll see what I can do. Pop, would you promise to let this go until I get back?"

"I'll do you one better. I'll pay for your flight if your mom can find a reasonable fare."

THE NEXT DAY, Julian flew over some incredible terrain he wished he could explore on his bike. The landscape was dotted with sparkling lakes and rivers. When the plane landed, Julian picked up a few brochures at the airport, almost forgetting this was more than a fishing trip.

He rented a Jeep and loaded his duffel and a case with his rod and reel. Before he'd left Georgia, he'd phoned Larry Adams, who offered his spare bedroom, but also said he was working odd hours undercover. Julian didn't mind at all—it gave him reason to find a motel near Garnet Patton's school. Being on his own also meant he had freedom to snoop. The men had agreed to meet whenever Larry found time to hoist a beer and shoot a little pool.

Julian had done some checking before leaving Georgia and had learned that the school where Ms. Patton taught was in session from August to mid-May. He'd have to work fast. He had no idea how the woman spent her summers. Maybe she taught summer school. But there was every possibility she'd leave Anchorage. He would if his kid had been stolen. He'd be combing the country every chance he got.

As a detective, Julian had played many roles. One of the more effective was posing as a reporter. He checked in to his motel, dug out a battered black notebook and drove to the school. The motel clerk had told him school let out at three.

He got there a little after and found a mass exodus of kids and cars leaving the fenced lot. "Hey," he called to several young men horsing around outside the front gate. "If a guy wanted to write an article on some of the more interesting teachers in your school, who might you suggest?"

"Whaddya mean by interesting?" asked the boy closest to Julian.

Julian opened his notebook. "I'm thinking along the lines of a human-interest story. Any of your teachers have stuff going on in their lives that would play to reader sympathy?"

The boys bandied about names, then settled on two—Mrs. Morrison and Ms. Patton. *Bingo!*

"You could go to the office and see one of the school secretaries if you want to talk to them. Mrs. Morrison, our science teacher, her husband got mauled real bad by a bear. It's been all over the paper for weeks. Haven't you seen it? He's probably gonna die. Mrs. Morrison's got a leave of absence."

Julian whistled sympathetically. "I agree, her story's probably been done enough. What's with… Ms. Patton, isn't that the other name you gave me?"

The boy, clearly the leader of the group, pointed behind Julian. "There she goes now to her car. And there's Ms. Cox, one of the secretaries. You can probably catch her. Ms. Patton's real sad because her stupid ex-husband snatched their kid a year or so ago. Their pictures were plastered all over town. Cops questioned everybody, but poof…the kid and her dad were gone."

Julian's gaze tracked the woman to an old Toyota. She was a surprise. Model-thin, she wore a conservative navy suit. Her longer-than-shoulder-length blond hair was combed back from a pale, oval face and clipped smoothly at her nape.

She stopped and checked all around before unlocking her car. Apparently satisfied no danger lurked nearby, she tossed her purse and bulging briefcase onto the passenger seat, then slid in the driver's side.

Murmuring his thanks to the helpful teens, Julian went in search of the secretary, Ms. Cox, even as Ms. Patton started her engine and drove off. He intercepted the secretary before she could leave the school grounds. Julian fed her the reporter story, and turned on the charm as he asked her about doing a feature on her colleague.

"You should probably talk to Garnet. I know she thinks no one cares about her case anymore. But at the same time, the publicity brought her a lot of unwanted attention. You know, from crazies."

Julian scribbled in his book while pumping the woman about the abduction.

"They were always an odd couple," she ventured. "Dale changed after he lost his job on the pipeline. He put on weight and let his hair get bushy. He also grew a scruffy beard and mustache. I heard he hung out with bikers. Oh, I probably shouldn't have said that. You won't print that, will you?" She looked worriedly up through her lashes.

Julian found the mention of bikers very interesting. He wanted to probe deeper, but the secretary began nervously edging away. He thanked her for her help, his mind stuck on Lee Hackett. Except for the biker connection, the two men didn't seem alike. Hackett wasn't a big man. "Don't worry. I'll consider our conversation off the record," he said with another disarming smile.

"Good. You really should talk to Garnet. Or her teacher friends. They're all in the hectic final days of classes. Oh, but earlier today I heard some of them planning to go to happy hour Friday at the Silver Springs Lounge. To celebrate turning in their grades. Garnet said she might go."

Julian tucked his notebook in his pocket. He wasn't at all sure he wanted to confront Garnet Patton. But just in case, he drove past the Silver Springs Lounge on his way back to the motel. It was an upscale establishment, and dark enough inside to allow for anonymous observations.

Eager to try out one of the local streams, Julian thought he'd get up early and fish Thursday morning. And maybe he'd spend the afternoon talking with Ms. Patton's neighbors. Maybe he wouldn't need a face-to-face meeting. Although he was curious to see how a woman with a missing daughter handled a night out on the town. Somehow, Julian didn't think too highly of the mother of a missing daughter who went about her life as if everything was status quo.

CHAPTER TWO

JULIAN RELAXED BY a lazy river. Before the morning mist evaporated he'd caught two rainbow trout. Beauties he was sorry to release. Hungry for fish, he stopped for a burger instead at a biker bar he passed on his way back to the motel. Inside, he struck up conversation with a cold-eyed bruiser seated at the counter. "Julian Cavenaugh, *North Alaska Tribune,*" he said, inventing a paper. "I'm considering a follow-up on the Dale Patton story. Ever heard of him?"

"Yeah. But why would anyone want to stir that up again?"

Julian bit into his burger and licked the juice that trickled down his thumb. "I'm curious how Patton managed to slip away, even though there must've been posters and stuff all over the state."

"So Dale's slippery. End of story. Find a new one, pal." Several tough guys in the room laughed.

The bruiser took a last slug from his beer, tossed money on the counter, hitched up his pants and left. At least five others followed him out.

Hearing the roar of bike engines from out front, Julian tried asking his waitress, but she didn't know Patton. She attempted to flirt, but Julian wasn't interested. He left his burger, paid his bill and returned to the motel to shower and change. He decided to try his luck with Garnet Patton's neighbors.

The first woman who answered his knock was treated to Julian's best smile. The fact that he petted the woman's fussy dog won him an audience with Anna Winkleman, senior citizen. "I'm writing a follow-up story on the missing Patton child," Julian fibbed after introducing himself and showing her his false credentials. "No doubt you've given accounts in the past, but I wondered if you'd mind talking about it again."

"Mercy, I'm grateful her case hasn't been forgotten. Poor Garnet's exhausted herself and spent every cent she doesn't absolutely need to live on, trying to find her precious baby. She's so discouraged. Is it possible to find Sophie after so long?"

Still petting the pooch, Julian considered how to answer. "Anything is possible," he finally said. "Mrs.

Winkleman, how well did you know Dale Patton? Is he the type who could've hurt his daughter to spite his ex? She did file for the divorce, correct?"

"She did. But Garnet moved here after the kidnapping. I never met Dale. All I really know about him is hearsay. Rumor is that he got in with a bunch of no-good bikers who drank and caroused. Other people say he took Sophie on his motorcycle when she was a toddler. He bought her a helmet, but still…I say Garnet did the right thing divorcing him."

"Was his taking their daughter for bike rides a big reason for the divorce?"

Anna looked blank. "I'm not sure. I believe it had some bearing on her seeking sole custody. But who can blame her? She said that about a month before she petitioned family court for sole custody, one of Dale's biker friends was struck and killed by a logging truck. It was obviously not appropriate for a child to be on one of those things. Then, a few days after the judge's ruling, before Garnet was able to get copies of the new court order to the school, Dale showed up at the preschool on his motorcycle and took off with Sophie."

Julian jotted notes in his book. "Thanks, you've

been very helpful. I'd like to talk to some of Ms. Patton's other friends. Can you suggest anyone?"

"Her friends in this building, you mean? Well, there's Hazel Webber downstairs, and John Carlyle, who lives next door to Garnet. However, I saw John leave to walk his dog. He has a rat terrier he takes up the street to the park. He'll probably be at a picnic table playing checkers with his cronies."

Giving Anna's dog a last pat, Julian went downstairs to find the Webber unit. He hit a roadblock with the white-haired matron who opened the door. She gazed haughtily down her nose at him. "I don't talk to nosy strangers, young man," she said before slamming her door.

Julian crossed her off his list and left in search of Mr. Carlyle and his rat terrier. He found them two blocks from the complex. Julian stopped, mumbled his name and said, "I hope, sir, that you won at checkers." He dived straight into his request for information on Garnet, hastily adding that Anna Winkleman had steered him this way.

"That busybody. Why can't you get what you need from your paper's archives? Ah, because you're no reporter. Sonny, I'd say you look more like a cop." Squinting, the old fellow studied Julian carefully. "Yes or no?"

Embarrassed at being found by the perceptive old man, Julian winced. Quickly, he showed him his badge, careful to explain that his role was strictly unofficial. "I'm just a cop who hates cold cases," he said, feeling guilty nevertheless. "Sometimes a fresh take on old information can lead to apprehensions," he added. That was true, and so was his next comment. "Some people feel intimidated by cops and are more comfortable talking to reporters."

"Huh, well, some cops lack basic people skills. Not saying that applies to you, young fella. Now, I never met Dale Patton, Garnet moved in next to me after the kidnapping. But my checkers partner knew him. He swears Dale loved that baby, too. Swede, that's my checkers buddy, lives on the other side of the park where the Pattons used to live. According to him, Dale felt shut out by Garnet's friends. They didn't think he was good enough for her. Swede said Dale dropped out of high school and came here from Washington State to work on the pipeline. A lot of young men did. When the jobs petered out, most went home. That's not easy for a married man, especially if his wife has a good job. Mind you,

Swede's never said Garnet and Dale fought over who brought in the bread. But I figure it'd be a sore subject, particularly if you add it to criticism by a wife's friends."

As they meandered back to the apartments, Julian drew some conclusions of his own. He thanked John, then left him with his terrier at the entrance. Once in his Jeep, Julian studied the new data on Patton. It fit his observations of Lee Hackett.

Julian's stomach tightened. Was his dad right this time? One stepson had said that Hackett once owned a motorcycle. Evidence pointed to Patton hanging with a biker crowd. The only fly in the ointment, so to speak, was that the school secretary's physical description of Dale Patton in no way matched Lee Hackett.

Even so, Julian wasn't ready to pack it in and go home. Instead, he made a second trip to the high school. This time he managed to bump into a pair of teachers who exited the building with Ms. Patton. He approached the two women after they left Garnet at her car, and they were plainly curious about him. The younger teacher, who introduced herself as Jenny Hoffman, immediately acted coy with Julian. The second woman gave her name as Molly

Eberhart, but neither seemed eager to talk to him about Garnet other than to defend her.

"Any man who'd steal a child from her mother is a creep. I never liked him," Jenny said scraping back her long hair. "Garnet's so far out of his league. The mystery is why she married him in the first place. Tracy Williams and I were right to voice our objections to him at the custody hearing. Look what he did."

"He had more decency than you and Tracy gave him credit for," Molly ventured.

"So he phoned the preschool and told the secretary Sophie was okay. He still waited two days and notice he phoned *before* the police tapped the line."

Molly tsked. "Jenny, that call kept Garnet from falling apart. I think she wishes she'd never asked for sole custody."

"You haven't seen Garnet cry her eyes out. She'll never be her old self until Sophie's back safe and Dale's behind bars."

Julian listened to the women sparring. He finally excused himself. "Ladies, I appreciate your insight. I guess I need to go read all the old articles," he said, carefully keeping the reporter persona intact.

Jenny caught up with him as he approached his

Jeep. "You can verify everything I said with Garnet. Sorry I didn't think to mention it earlier, but a small group of us are going to the Silver Springs lounge to celebrate the end of school. I'll introduce you two. Just remember, I saw you first."

"All I'm after are some unbiased opinions."

"Huh, you won't find any friend of Garnet's with an unbiased opinion."

Julian offered a smile as he climbed into in his Jeep. He had, in fact, found two unbiased opinions. One belonged to Molly Eberhart, the other to John Carlyle. Tossing off a wave, Julian pulled out of his parking space. He spent the next hour at the library poring over old records. The story had been front-page news for months, then, as was typical, it tapered to nothing when leads fell off.

Julian shut down his laptop and thanked the archive specialist. He dropped his stuff at the motel. Then, because Larry Adams had left a message to meet him at a nearby pub, Julian dashed out again.

Lingering in the doorway of the smoky, noisy bar, Julian let his eyes adjust while trying to pinpoint the cop he'd met only twice before.

Larry recognized him, came over and slapped him on the shoulder.

"Wow, I'd never have known you if I'd bumped into you on the street," Julian said.

"That's the point of an undercover disguise," Larry said, leading Julian to a booth at the back of the pub where two beers sat in sweaty mugs. He slid in first, and Julian took the opposite bench. "What's up in Atlanta? Are they fresh out of crime? With your workaholic reputation, I never expected you to make it to my neck of the woods."

Taking a swig of cold beer, Julian shrugged. "It's my reward for finally nailing a sleazebag who terrorized women in one of our burbs for over four months." He went on to describe the case in more detail.

Larry spun his mug, staring at the wet rings it left on the tabletop. "I'm glad I work Narc now. I had to get out of Violent Crimes. How'd you keep from plugging a guy like that and claiming he tried to escape? We had one recently who walked on a technicality."

"It happens. My partner's a twenty-year man who lost his oldest daughter to a repeat offender. He and I go the extra mile to make sure our collars are by-the-book so our evidence holds up."

"That's good. Alaska courts have been known to

accept that our citizens are entitled to a wild and woolly lifestyle. Or maybe we attract more than our share of renegades and malcontents." The topic trailed off as Larry perused a worn menu.

As Julian picked up his own, he considered asking Larry if he knew anything about the Patton kidnapping. It'd help to get a professional opinion on whether Dale Patton was one of the malcontents or renegades. But he'd already risked too much nosing into a case that wasn't his. And unless his father's hunch was correct, the case would never be under his jurisdiction. Taking another slug of beer, Julian decided against involving a casual friend.

ALTHOUGH SHE'D NEVER stopped grieving the loss of her missing child, Garnet Patton didn't live in a fog. She'd seen the good-looking, dark-haired stranger hanging around outside her school. Strangers on campus often meant drug deals. Yesterday, when she saw him speak to some of her better students, her antennae had shot up. She hadn't seen anything change hands and he hadn't stuck around, so she felt all right about driving away. In class today she'd asked the students. They said the guy was a reporter.

She was surprised to hear from neighbors that a

similar man had questioned them about her. Anna Winkleman from across the hall also said he was a reporter. He'd gotten nowhere with Hazel Webber.

So, who was he and what was really going on? It was definitely strange, but at least no one found him threatening. Which was why she didn't totally freak out when her best friend, Jenny Hoffman, phoned and announced that very same guy had returned to campus and questioned her and Molly Eberhart. "I think it's funny he hasn't talked to you, Garnet. He said he's a reporter, but Molly thinks he's a cop or maybe FBI. That's pure speculation, though."

A ripple of hope ran through Garnet, which she quickly reined in. "Why do you suppose he didn't come to me instead of poking about? If someone new has been assigned to Sophie's case I would've expected Sergeant Savage to tell me."

"Gary Savage is an arrogant SOB, Garnet. It would kill him to share a case."

Garnet was used to Jenny's dismissing the sergeant. "Hmm. And why would the department let a new man go over old ground?"

"The new guy is *so* hot, whoever he is. Very yummy! By the way, I invited him to come by the Silver Springs tomorrow after school."

Garnet's heart sped up. "He's coming?"

"He didn't say yes, but he didn't say no, either. I'm giving fair warning. If he shows up I have dibs on him."

"Jenny! If he's reopening my case, don't distract him. Oh, but…I'm getting way ahead of myself. Could they have a lead on Dale? Gary told me months ago that all the tips had dried up. I wonder…"

"Don't. Guessing doesn't get you anywhere. Isn't that what we tell our students? I'd hate to see you get your hopes up, Garnet. What if he really is a reporter?"

"I can't help myself. Sophie should start first grade in September. From the day she was born I imagined how we'd mark each milestone in her life. Like starting school, going on her first date, graduating and…" Garnet's voice broke.

"Don't torture yourself, Garnet. Anyway, I have to go—I've got a date in fifteen minutes with Steve the Stud."

"On a school night?" Garnet dragged her thoughts back to her friend. "Are you and Steve getting serious?"

"Are you kidding? I can't get serious about a man

whose ego is bigger than his IQ. And before you say *Jenny* in that shocked tone, let me say Steve knows the score. I love having a man around. That's why I hit on the new guy. Would you believe it, Garnet? Neither Molly nor I got his name. Mr. Yummy has that lean, hungry look that appeals to my baser instincts. I suppose it's too much to hope he's more intelligent than most of the men we meet."

"Jenny, you are so bad. Steve's no dummy. If you're going to date him, you should give him a little respect. It takes skill to be a good plumber."

"Mama and Daddy wouldn't let him past their front door." Jenny sighed.

"If you'd wanted to live by their standards, you'd still be in Chicago. You can't please them and yourself, Jenny. I came to Alaska for the same reasons. Isn't it time you stopped spinning at the end of their rope?"

"Oh, right, like I'd want the heartache marrying Dale Patton brought you. I'll romp with bad boys, but when I marry someone, he'll have read something other than the Sunday comics, and he'll know which fork to pick up first at a banquet."

The hum of the dial tone told Garnet Jenny had hung up in a huff. They'd met in college. Garnet's dad was a self-absorbed astronomer, Jenny's father, the president of an elite private school. Both sets of parents were livid when their daughters went off to Alaska, a state many Easterners still thought was uncivilized.

Garnet's family hadn't spoken to her since she'd announced her intent to marry Dale, who'd worked on the pipeline then. They'd had a couple of good years, but Garnet had to admit that the man she'd fallen in love with had changed drastically after he lost his job. Her friends believed their arguments were all about Dale's newfound biker buds. But Garnet didn't object to his motorcycle. There was a time she'd loved riding on his bike. She'd thought Dale's pirate looks added to his charm. Under the tough veneer was a soft-spoken gentleman, until suddenly he seemed to do a one-eighty turn. Certainly he'd been upset over losing his job; he hated not being the family provider. Add that to her friends' attitude. Looking back, she accepted that the divorce had been partly her fault. Still, the last thing Garnet expected from the man she'd loved, shared her innermost feelings—and a child—with, was that he'd deal her the most hurtful blow a mother could ever experience.

She realized she was still clutching the phone. She dialed Sergeant Savage from memory. A dispatcher answered. "This is Garnet Patton. Could I speak to Gary Savage please?"

There was a brief pause before Sergeant Savage came on.

Garnet plunged straight into the reason for her call. When she'd finished, the silence went on so long she thought the connection had broken. As she was about to hang up and redial, Savage cleared his throat. "Sorry, Garnet, you took me by surprise. We haven't hired any new officers, nor have we had any new tips on Dale. I know school's nearly out. May I suggest using your break to get out of Anchorage? Leave a number where I can reach you and I'll be in touch if anything comes up. I'll reiterate what I said before. I have the necessary controls in place. I believe we'll find Sophie. Dale will get careless, or he'll be arrested for something else and his prints will crop up in a database. Just be patient, my dear."

Garnet *im*patiently waited for Sergeant Savage to finish his spiel. "If this guy isn't from your department, who is he? My students think he's a reporter. Other people say he has cop written all over him."

"We've talked about how there'll be people

coming out of the woodwork in cases like yours. Some have a mean streak, and some believe they'll be able to do what cops haven't. Then there are psychics who set out to either test their so-called powers or wait in the wings until the victims get desperate enough to hire them. Tell you what, Garnet, I'll put out feelers around town. But I'm betting this joker falls into one of those categories. Can you give me a description?"

She offered one to the best of her memory, and heard the scratch of Gary's pen.

"Be careful, Garnet. A few of these jerks are pure nuts. Rest assured, if anything new turns up I'll let you know. If you set eyes on this imposter again, phone dispatch. I'll leave a standing order to bring him in."

Garnet hung up, more discouraged than ever. She knew there were people who preyed on the misfortunes of others. The fact remained—there'd been nothing alarming about the man she'd glimpsed at school. Anna Winkleman used the word *charming* to describe him. And Jenny…but Jenny had different criteria.

It might be a mistake, but Garnet decided if she saw the stranger again she'd have a word with him before phoning dispatch.

Her nerves had frayed and she found it difficult to concentrate on doing the math necessary to average final grades. Maybe a walk would clear her head. She shrugged into a sweater coat to block the chill in the air, and left her apartment.

John Carlyle stepped into the hallway as Garnet pocketed her key. "Hello, Garnet. Going out? I'm taking Hoover for his nightly walk."

The rotund little terrier was so named because he inhaled any scrap of food that landed on the floor. Hoover loved people and had a particular fondness for Garnet, who gave him nutritious doggie treats. She felt in her pocket and came up with a couple of small lint-covered dog biscuits. "Mind if I tag along?" she asked.

"We'd be pleased. Mr. Hoover thanks you for his treats. Is something wrong with your car? You don't usually go walking."

After rubbing the wriggling animal's backside, Garnet straightened and led the way to the stairs. "Sophie used to love going on walks, John. I tend to avoid the activities we did together."

"Understandable."

She heaved a sigh. "Not everyone agrees. I just spoke with the officer heading up my case. He's adamant about me getting on with my life." She stepped aside at the main door and let the courtly old gentleman open the door for her.

"Oh. So that bright young fellow I met today—the new cop on your case—he didn't find anything new?"

Garnet stopped. "You saw him? I thought Anna Winkleman and Hazel Webber were the only ones home when he came by. Anna said you'd taken Hoover to the park. John, what did that man say? Did he give his name? You see, Sergeant Savage said there was no new cop on my case."

"Really?" Tugging back on Hoover's leash, Mr. Carlyle stroked his chin thoughtfully. "I'm sure he told me his name. His badge certainly looked legit." The old man's face fell. "My hearing's not what it used to be, Garnet. I'm sorry, I didn't catch everything he said. His name was…Irish, maybe? Should I not have talked to him?"

She walked on, shortening her stride to match his. "Truthfully, John, I suppose he's a curiosity seeker at best and at worst, who knows? A con man, probably. In the morning I'll give you a number you can call if he comes around again. Savage said they'd take him in and find out what he's up to." She paused while Hoover sniffed a hydrant.

"I've always had a good radar for crooks. This fellow, whatever he is, he's pretty convincing. I s'pose you're teaching summer school again? I know you need the money and want to keep busy, but I hate seeing you so thin. You're practically skin and bones."

Her low chuckle had a catch at the end. "Actually, I'm not teaching this summer. I don't know what I'll do, John. I do need to fill every hour of the day but I'm burning out emotionally. I won't be any good to next year's students unless I back off for awhile. I hear pulling fishnets is a physically demanding job. It might be the distraction I need. Maybe I'll drive down to Ketchikan and see if I can sign on with a salmon vessel."

"Huh, I'd think twice about that. I spent a couple of summers during my college days on a crab boat. A stinkier, dirtier job only exists if you get stuck in one of the canneries. Darlene's Café has a sign in the window for a waitress. I'm there at least once a week. Never been in the place that every seat isn't taken. Wouldn't pay what teaching does, or fishing, but it'd be a change of pace and safer than going to sea with a rough-and-tumble fishing crew."

"Thanks for the tip. I'll consider it. Maybe I'll go by this weekend and talk to Darlene. Teaching ends this week. The kids are out tomorrow, but we have three days to clean up."

John looked pleased that he could help. Then, as darkness fell and a misty drizzle started, they turned back, picking up their pace.

Garnet studied the cars that passed, and she took a longer look at those parked near the apartment complex.

John noticed. "You expecting a visitor tonight?"

"No. It's nothing. I'm sure this stranger doesn't know anything. Yet it's been ages since our law enforcement has received a tip no matter how slim, I guess I held out hope. Silly, I know."

Mr. Carlyle picked up his dog and opened the front door. "Not silly at all. So, for the next few days at least, if you want to walk after dark, call me. Not to scare you or anything."

She gave an involuntary shudder. "The teachers have planned an after-school happy hour tomorrow at the Silver Springs Lounge. I didn't commit, but Jenny Hoffman—you know her—told me she met the stranger and invited him to join us for drinks."

John caught Garnet's elbow. "Maybe you shouldn't go. Whatever you do, don't let him separate you from your friends. The lounge has a doorman. If you feel threatened, ask him to escort you to your car."

"This is dumb." She tossed her head, as though shaking off her anxiety. "I'll be fine. I really doubt anyone wanting to hurt me would show his face in such a public venue. Frankly, the guy probably got his kicks and is long gone. Good night, John. Thanks for caring. I'll be fine."

ALL THE NEXT DAY, Garnet periodically glanced out her classroom window. At lunch, she sat on the front steps, all but daring the man in the Jeep to appear. No rust-red Jeep materialized any time that afternoon, either.

The bell rang, signaling the end of the school day—and the year. Students streamed into Garnet's room to say their final goodbyes. At four o'clock, Jenny stuck her head in the room.

"What did you decide about happy hour? I'm riding with Wendy and Susan. You want to hitch? Wendy can drop you off back here to pick up your car."

"No, thanks. I'll drive on my own. I have a couple of things to tidy up here. Order me a Cosmopolitan, will you?"

"Oooh, you're going whole hog. I think I'll get one, too."

Twenty minutes later, Garnet scanned the street between the school and her car. Still no Jeep. Nor was one parked near the lounge. She got lucky and found a parking place right outside the front door.

The last to arrive, Garnet slipped onto a stool Jenny had saved. The friends laughed, joked, toasted each other, and helped themselves to a variety of hors d' oeuvres. A few teachers left, but Garnet had ordered a second drink when Jenny slid off her stool to leave with Wendy. "I'm seriously bummed," she said. "The hottie's a no-show. Come on, Garnet, we'll walk you to your car."

Garnet waved them away. "I'm parked right next to the door. I'll be fine, Jenny. Considering what I paid for this drink I'm not wasting a drop. I think I'll find a booth and order some dinner. I'll see you Monday. We need to talk about what we're going to do over the summer break." Standing, Garnet hugged all three friends. The trio walked out and Garnet signaled a waiter to request a booth. He carried her drink, put it down and said, "I'll bring you a menu."

"No need. I'll just have a chicken Caesar salad."

The waiter turned away. Garnet started to sit, but felt as if she were being watched. Not uncommon. The lounge was a popular hangout.

A quick glance around the room, though, and she froze. A man who must've just entered was indeed staring at her. It was the stranger who'd been asking questions at school and her apartment complex. Garnet's cheeks heated as he blatantly slid a sleepy-lidded gaze from her head to her toes and back again.

SOMEHOW, once Julian saw Jenny and the other women leave, he didn't expect to find Garnet Patton inside. When he did spot her, he didn't think she'd recognize him. But the instant their eyes met and he watched her square her slim shoulders and narrow her eyes, Julian knew he'd been made. He considered ducking out, although perhaps it was time to discover if her ex-husband might have a reason to be setting up housekeeping in Georgia.

Besides, from the set of her jaw as she marched toward him, she plainly had questions of her own, and she intended to get answers.

CHAPTER THREE

"WHO ARE YOU?" Garnet demanded, nervously tugging down the sleeves of her sweater. "Why are you asking questions about me?"

Julian started to hedge his answer. But the light-bulbs around the bar mirror highlighted the fragile shadows under her eyes, indicating she was far more vulnerable than the rigid set of her spine suggested.

"I'm Julian Cavenaugh. I'm a detective from Atlanta," he explained, noting her deepening frown. At this point, Julian was hoping to see a spark of rec-ognition, something to indicate she'd heard of the area. Nothing was forthcoming. Instead, she shook her head, loosening strands of pale hair from a silver clip at her neck.

"I'm afraid I still don't understand."

And Julian could see she didn't. "Please, won't you sit down? I'll try to explain. As well, I think your waiter lost you. The poor guy's looking confused.

I'd hate to be responsible for him taking your dinner back to the kitchen."

His soft drawl and winsome smile caused Garnet to look back at her booth. Giving an ever-so slight nod, she made her way through the crowded room to her table. She apologized to her waiter.

"I saw your jacket was still here," he said, beaming. "Is there anything else I can get you, miss?" He set her salad down and shook open a snowy linen napkin. Then he apparently noticed Julian hovering to his left.

Garnet sat and reluctantly motioned to the opposite seat. "Please bring the gentleman a menu." She eyed her drink, then pushed the glass aside, and said, "I'd like coffee, please. Black."

"I'll take a dark ale. Whatever's on tap." Julian closed the menu. "I'd like your best steak with whatever fixings it comes with." Offering Garnet another smile, he added, "Can I talk you into ordering something more substantial than rabbit food and high-octane caffeine? I promise I don't mean you any harm. I haven't bitten anyone since I was three. Suzie Walker from down the street. And she bit me first, and harder."

Arching an eyebrow, Garnet moved croutons

aside with her fork and spread the fresh Parmesan. "My salad is loaded with chicken, which won't clog my arteries. I'd point out you don't know anything about me or my habits, good or bad, but that's not true, is it, Mr. Cavenaugh? You've been asking my friends a lot of personal questions."

"Julian, please." He had the grace to look embarrassed.

His beer came and they both fell silent a moment. "So, you're a cop, not a reporter?" Garnet continued to pick at her salad, and Julian fidgeted with his cutlery and the salt and pepper shakers. He showed her his badge, returning it to his jacket pocket distractedly.

As his silence dragged on, Garnet worried that once again she'd pinned her hopes on a stranger who would disappoint her. Long ago, Garnet had vowed she'd risk everything, even meet with the devil himself if it would lead to her daughter's whereabouts.

Now, as she studied the man seated across from her—his hawkish features and black hair curling stubbornly over his ears—she thought it was entirely possible she'd done exactly that.

"I don't quite know where to start," Julian said, tracing a line down the damp glass with his finger.

Garnet set down her fork and clasped her hands to keep them still. "Please, oh, please, if this has anything to do with Sophie just tell me straight out."

Affected by her ragged voice, Julian looked away and drank from his beer. He dug in his shirt pocket and removed the grainy photograph he'd taken of the little Hackett girl at her front window. The one where he'd caught her in partial profile. He slid the snapshot across the table.

Garnet snatched it up with a strangled cry. Questions poured out one after another. "When, ah, where? How? It's so unclear. *Is* this Sophie?"

Trying to tread carefully, Julian leaned forward. "What do you think?"

"Oh, God. I wish I could be sure. This was taken from too far away." She placed the picture gently on the table. "It's been over a year. That day, I let her dress herself for preschool. She chose pink cords, a frilly white blouse and bright red sneakers. At lunchtime, my ex-husband arrived at Sophie's preschool unannounced. He barged past office staff who knew he shouldn't have access and took her. The last time I saw her was when I dropped her off. In my dreams, she looks exactly as she did then. Realistically, I know she's changed. She's probably lost her baby fat."

Julian said nothing, letting Garnet fill the silence. "Dale—my ex—and I finalized a bitter second custody hearing two days before he kidnapped her. The police think the fact that I was given full custody set him off. Friends said they'd seen Dale drinking excessively. Someone had witnessed him losing his temper." Tears filled her eyes as she picked up the photo and caressed it with her thumb. "Why would you make the trip from Georgia to Alaska to show me a fuzzy photo? You called yourself a detective. Are you a private detective? Who hired you? Wayne Jenkins is the last P.I. I paid to find Sophie. He stopped his search when I couldn't scrape together his monthly retainer. Did he approach you for some reason?"

"No. I have nothing to do with Wayne Jenkins." Pausing to accept his steak and assure the waiter that the meat was cooked to his liking, Julian swallowed a small bite. He needed to tread cautiously. He hadn't intended to reveal his reason for meddling in her life, but because she'd obviously been hurt in the past, he decided to share a bit more of his background. "I work for the Atlanta PD. But I'm on vacation. The truth is I have absolutely no official status in your case."

She stared at him from teary eyes.

Julian shifted under her gaze. "Uh, my parents live in a small town about thirty miles outside Atlanta. Pop's a postman nearing retirement. Part of his job…" Julian hesitated before continuing. "Part of his job is delivering cards that feature pictures of missing children. Pop loves kids, so he takes it very seriously." Julian sawed off a piece of steak and stabbed it with his fork. He had no idea how fiercely he glared at it until Garnet reached across and tentatively touched his hand.

"The sergeant handling my case contacted the organization that does the postcards. We worked with them and the FBI for several months. I'm told they never close the book on a case until a missing child turns up safely…or dead," she whispered, punctuating her obvious worry with a sob.

"Stop that," Julian pleaded. "I'm trying to say my dad has a file box full of those cards. He sees any new families on his route, he keeps an eye open. But here's the kicker. Once, a long time ago, when my brothers, my sister and I were in school, Pop was sure he'd found a boy on one of those cards. He was dead wrong, and a lot of people got real upset."

"Are you trying to say that your father saw

Sophie's card and…and thinks the child in this photograph is her?"

Julian heard the hope in her voice, and tried not to encourage it. "What I'm telling you is that Pop was way off the mark the other time he thought he was right. A lot of people in our town, my family included, were adversely affected. I'm older and wiser now, and in a better position to protect him from making another mistake. Do you understand what I mean?"

"Yes, of course." She made the appropriate response, but Julian could tell she'd grabbed on to the notion and had already let it grow by leaps and bounds.

"Eat," he ordered, pointing at her virtually untouched salad with his steak knife. Scowling, he dug in to his baked potato and vegetables.

Garnet grabbed her fork and began spearing lettuce like a dutiful child. She even managed to swallow some, despite finding it difficult to remain still.

Her hopefulness kept Julian from bringing out the second photo—the one of a happily smiling Lee Hackett dancing around his garage with his equally joyous daughter. The little girl this lovely woman across from him wanted to be her missing Sophie.

"Before you get too invested in this," Julian said seriously, "there are other questions that need to be considered. For instance, does your husband, uh, Sophie's father, have relatives or friends living in the south?"

Her face fell, but she rallied to say coolly, "Dale is my ex-husband, and I'm not aware if he has family outside of Washington, but I'll call his mother. His parents live in an assisted-living center in Washington State. An older brother farms in the Skagit Valley, also in Washington. What friends he has live here in Anchorage. But I'm the custodial parent and Dale took Sophie against a court order allowing him only supervised visits. If you know where he is, isn't it your duty as a law officer to arrest him for kidnapping?"

"Yes. *If* it's your daughter in the snapshot. That's a big if."

For the first time, Garnet realized this man had her at a disadvantage. Other than claiming to have come from Atlanta, Detective Cavenaugh had been very careful to give nothing away. Nothing Garnet could use to track Sophie on her own.

"I officially finish work for the summer next Wednesday," she said. "I'll book a flight tomorrow if you'll tell me where I can see her for myself." She stared at the photograph, as if willing the picture to sharpen.

"Oh, right," Julian drawled. "And if it is her, what's to stop your ex from murdering you and taking off with her again?"

"Dale would never do that." She lifted her chin defiantly and drilled him with her eyes.

"Excuse me, I thought you told me he had a temper."

"A… One coworker said she saw him lose it after I petitioned for divorce. I only ever saw moodiness. That started after he was laid off from his job and couldn't find work. I was pregnant with Sophie at the time."

"So, you two *didn't* fight?"

She fiddled with her knife. "That depends on your definition of fighting. Dale thought we should pack up and go to Washington. Move in with his brother. But he had no job prospects there, so I balked at quitting my teaching job. I have tenure, plus my job provided us with insurance, and we had a baby due."

Julian finished his potato while contemplating her last statement. "I wish you'd eat," he said, making it clear he intended to clean his plate. "If this is all you normally eat, you won't last a day on the hunt. Georgia is three thousand miles from here."

"Then…you'll tell me where to find this little girl?"

When Julian didn't answer immediately, Garnet hurriedly ate what she could. "Now you've clammed up. Talk to me," she begged, knuckles white around her fork. "Tell me everything you know about her, please."

"That's not much," he muttered. "The mother in the household and one of two school-age boys supposedly told a neighbor that their sister suffers from asthma. I wasn't able to verify that."

"Sophie was never sick a day in her life. And… there's a mother?" Garnet held her breath and let it out slowly. "Are you saying Dale has remarried? Did you look for a marriage certificate?"

"You're jumping to conclusions. First of all, this family isn't using the name Patton. Second, the boys have yet another last name. They haven't been in town long." He picked up his beer. "I did check. There's no record of this man and woman being issued a marriage license in Georgia. Tell me, does it bother you that your ex might have a new woman? One of your teacher friends said you and he were mismatched and that your marriage was a mistake from the get-go."

Garnet stared at her plate. "Dale and I met at a housewarming party seven years ago. We were twenty-two. I'm an only child and my parents both had demanding careers that took up a lot of their time. You could say we had a chilly household. One day, shortly after graduation, my college roommate, Jenny, suggested we send résumés to Alaska. I was beyond ready to leave Chicago. I met Dale during that…exploratory phase in my life."

She balled up her napkin. "He was the antithesis of any man I'd dated before. I can't deny we shared some good years—before he began saying I was obsessive about wanting a healthy savings account to ensure Sophie's security."

Garnet's tone tightened. "I wonder if he knows I emptied that savings account in six months searching for him. I doubt he'd care that I had to sell the house and move to an efficiency apartment. In the move, I kept Sophie's favorite toys, but gave her clothes to a local church. Mostly, I couldn't bear the reminder that at the end of a year she would've outgrown everything."

Julian polished off his beer and waited to see if

Garnet would volunteer tidbits that would ring any bells. Apparently, she'd reached her limit. And it bothered him to see the raw emotion in her haunted eyes.

"Did you keep any pictures of your ex-husband?"

"I'm not sure. I threw a lot of stuff away. What about this man in Georgia? Can you describe him?"

The photo of Hackett burned a hole in Julian's shirt pocket, but he wasn't ready to produce it. Instead, he gave a brief description of what he recalled of the little girl's father.

Garnet's shoulders slumped. "It's not Dale. He was slightly less blond than me—his beard, mustache and hair were hard to tame. No one would describe him as wiry. More like burly. After he fell in with the biker set he bulked up a lot. Picture your typical biker. Leather pants, jacket with wide silver zippers and a bandana tied around bushy hair. That's Dale."

The information interested Julian. Hackett had been keen to examine his Ducati. As well, one of the boys had indicated their stepdad had owned a bike. Julian folded his napkin. "Some of those characteristics could be altered. I wouldn't mind taking a look at a picture of him if you have one."

Garnet put down her coffee cup. She had time to mull over Julian's request as the waiter handed him the check. "I'll pay for my own," she rushed to say, picking up her purse. "Could you separate out my charges?" she asked the waiter.

"No need." Julian held up a hand. "I barged in on you and interrupted your dinner. It's only fair that I ante up." He took out his wallet and counted out enough to cover the bill and tip.

"Thank you," Garnet said softly, sliding to the edge of her seat.

Julian stood when she did. "Are you avoiding my question because you really can't remember if you have a picture of Dale, or because you don't want me following you home? If it's the latter, remember I've already been to your building. I spoke with your neighbors. It's not so late that I'd feel bad about asking one of them to chaperone." He winked.

"I guess I *have* become too suspicious since Sophie disappeared. I'm sure you're who you say you are."

"Hey, there's no need to apologize for not wanting to invite a stranger home. I wish all young women were as cautious."

"I'm not that young. Twenty-nine," she said primly.

"That old?" he drawled, resting a hand at her waist as he guided her to the door. "I have four years on you." He stopped outside the lounge in the glare of the neon sign and pulled out his wallet. He removed his Georgia driver's license and his police ID. He handed them to her and then, for good measure, he even produced a dog-eared library card.

She laughed at that, but relaxed noticeably. "Come on, then. Just so you know, Mr. Carlyle will make sure I'm safe and sound. He has excellent hearing and will poke his nose out the minute I put my key in the lock. I'll grant you his dog doesn't look dangerous, but I've seen Hoover take a bite out of the meter reader."

"That little porker? I might buy him beating an intruder to death with his tail. Round as he is, though, Carlyle must've named him for J. Edgar. They've definitely got the same physique."

"I should've realized you'd met Hoover. For your information, his name comes from the vacuum cleaner, not J. Edgar. For the way he licks up crumbs from under Mr. Carlyle's table."

"Hoover. That's rich. Hey, where are you parked? I'll walk you to your car."

Garnet pointed to the blue Toyota directly in front

of them. For emphasis, she aimed her automatic door opener and made the horn honk and lights flash.

"Ah, some detective I am. I saw you get into that car twice at school, yet I never noticed it right in front of me." He opened her door.

"Thanks, I'm not used to such service. I have assigned parking in the apartment garage. You'll have to park on the street if you can find a spot. I'll go inside from the garage. Press the buzzer by the front entrance and I'll let you in."

"The door wasn't locked when I made my rounds of your neighbors."

"It's open during the day, and automatically locks again in the evening. We have camera surveillance twenty-four hours a day. That's one reason I selected that particular apartment."

Julian thought he saw her shiver. He nodded, then shut the door after her. He supposed she'd always wish she'd had better surveillance on her daughter the day Dale Patton waltzed into that school and whisked her away. Julian felt sympathy for victims. He could imagine himself in their shoes. He wasn't a father, but he pictured how devastated his sister or his brothers would be under similar circumstances.

Turning onto Garnet's block fifteen minutes later, Julian considered the other half of the equation. How desperate would parents have to be to step outside the law and take off with their kid? They would be forever looking over a shoulder—always aware that one wrong move could land them in prison. And the child would be even more lost to them than before. Julian was so deep in thought he almost drove past Garnet's building.

Slowing, he saw a red pickup pull out of a spot close to the building's entrance. He zipped into the slot and vaulted out of the car. Bounding up the steps, he rang the bell and stepped into full view of the peephole.

"Goodness, you must've run some lights to get here so fast," Garnet exclaimed, nearly hitting him as she pushed open the door.

He gestured over his shoulder toward his Jeep. "Luck of the Irish. Somebody drove out as I approached."

"Do you mind if we take the stairs? I got stuck in an elevator once and was forced to endure five hours with a hysterical woman."

"No problem. After the meal I put away I could use the exercise." He patted his belly.

Garnet avoided looking but she couldn't help noticing that his abs were perfectly flat. She led the way up three flights of carpeted stairs. As she'd predicted, almost the moment she unlocked her door, the one to the right of hers opened. Balding Mr. Carlyle poked his head into the hall.

"There you are! I was getting worried. Your phone has rung three or four times. Oh, I didn't realize you had a guest, Garnet. How are you, Detective?" The spotted terrier nosed out and sniffed the air. Before Julian could answer, Hoover wiggled through the doorway and dashed up to jump excitedly between him and Garnet.

"He probably smells the steak I ate at the restaurant. I should've saved him some leftovers," Julian said, patting the dog's fat sides.

"So Detective…uh, what *is* your last name?"

"Cavenaugh."

"I hope you haven't brought Garnet bad news. I got to thinking that maybe your snooping into a case Sergeant Savage dropped the ball on didn't bode well for her."

Garnet started to speak, but Julian cut in. He didn't want her to sound too optimistic in the event the kid in Georgia wasn't Sophie. "I'm conducting a routine follow-up is all. Ms. Patton is going to show me a photograph of her ex. I know she appreciates you watching out for her, John."

"I was in the kitchen and heard her key. Hoover and I had just shared a tuna sandwich."

"You like fish, do you?" Julian glanced at the man. "Maybe you'd like a mess of fresh fish tomorrow night. I'm going fishing with a friend in the morning. I can't cook at my motel, and my friend works screwy hours and doesn't have the time."

The old man's eyes lit up. "That would be right nice. It's sockeye season. I can't afford to buy any on my pension. I know several people in the building would love a salmon feed."

"Sockeye? I don't think my friend planned to ocean fish, but maybe I'll suggest seeing if we can book passage on a charter boat."

"You catch anything after noon, you can find me at the park beating Swede Jensen at checkers." Carlyle scooped up his dog, touched two fingers to his temple and went inside his apartment. They heard the rattle of his safety chain.

Garnet shoved open her door and flipped on the light. "That was kind of you to offer him fish. He retired from lumbering a long time ago and he has to watch every penny. Do you think you'll catch a salmon? If so, I'll cook it for you both."

"Oh." Julian bit his lower lip.

"What's wrong?"

"Nothing. I spotted what looks like a good Italian restaurant not far from the lounge. I was going to ask you to join me there tomorrow evening."

"If it's Torinos, I'd be tempted to accept, Detective. It's one of my favorites. They serve the all-around best food in this part of town."

"I believe that was it. Two blocks down from the lounge."

"Right. Well, it's a nice thought, but I've been thinking of asking my principal if I can work Saturday and Sunday boxing up my classroom, and take two extra days as personal time off in order to leave for Georgia sooner."

"Hmm." Julian frowned. "Let's not get ahead of ourselves. We're still not certain it's them. Could we look for a photo of your ex to check?"

"Of course, please have a seat. On the way home, I remembered where I put the album my class gave us as a wedding gift. It has wedding photos and others taken during the early, happier years of our marriage." She steered Julian to a spot on the couch under a floor lamp so he could better see the album when she found it. Crossing the room, Garnet knelt at a cabinet.

Using the time to study his surroundings, Julian realized the area of paneling between the built-ins hid a Murphy bed. Garnet had called her place an efficiency apartment and she sure hadn't been kidding. There was a small kitchen tucked into one corner.

She didn't have a lot of furnishings or bric-a-brac. On every available surface and two walls were pictures of a sweet-faced child he knew had to be Sophie.

Rising, he picked up a four-photo frame that sat atop a narrow bookcase. The first was of a yawning infant lying on a blanket. In the second, Sophie was almost hidden behind a cake with one blazing candle. The third showed a toddler laughing and banging a toy on a high-chair tray. Julian spent longer studying the final photograph—a child of two or three. Her angelic smile was so very like her mother's, but Garnet's face was slimmer. Sophie's long hair curled in ringlets while Garnet pulled hers straight. The girl's hair was powder-white. After a glance at the woman across the room, Julian thought he'd call Garnet's shade more palomino.

Straining to recall the color of the Hackett girl's hair, Julian cursed his inability to recreate specifics. He thought she was blond but he couldn't swear to it. He'd been captivated by the twin expressions of delight on the faces of father and daughter and hadn't paid attention to much else. Now he felt guilty because that print was in his shirt pocket and he hadn't shared it with Garnet, even though she'd trusted him enough to let him into her home. He turned away from the photos and returned to the couch.

"Here it is," she exclaimed, dragging a white box out of the cabinet. She set it aside and replaced stacks of what looked like school texts and expandable file folders. Julian watched her work at the simple task and was surprised when he focused on the curve of her pale cheek and the movement of her hands. He found himself attracted and stirred in a way he hadn't anticipated.

Julian shifted uncomfortably.

Garnet rose gracefully and caught him scowling as she bent to retrieve the album. "Is something wrong, Detective?"

"What?" He jerked his head up. "Nothing," he muttered, knowing it was a lie. "It's getting late, let's have a look."

She lifted the album out of the box and leafed through several pages. "I seem to have more pictures of our wedding and reception than I remembered." She set the book in Julian's hands.

"Will you sit?" he snapped, suddenly aware of her as not a victim, but as a woman. Squeezing his eyes shut, he rubbed the lids, trying to clear his mind before he studied the prints. He did his best to ignore those shots of Garnet. She looked like an angel in the white strapless gown she'd worn to marry the jerk, Dale Patton.

There he went again. Julian was a detective who usually tried hard not to prejudge a suspect. And Patton wasn't even *his* suspect.

"What do you think?" Garnet asked anxiously, after Julian flipped past the reception shots to party pictures taken in a backyard.

"You described him well. I admit I'm having a hard time imagining you two together."

"I meant, do you think Dale is the man from your father's mail route?" She jerked the album out of Julian's hands and held it to her chest. A sigh escaped her lips. "Your assessment's not new. The local cops said the same thing after he took Sophie. Frankly, I don't see why I should have to explain that while Dale looks rough, he was gentle and funny when we met. He changed gradually, after he lost his job. But he still doted on Sophie, and he fell into the role of househusband while I worked. That's partly why I didn't file for a divorce right away. It's difficult to admit to failing at something so personal. I wanted to hold my marriage together. I didn't want friends, or worse, my parents, to say I'd chosen a partner unwisely," she said bitterly. "Then he began staying out nights partying, and cashed checks on the household account he neglected to mention. Friends saw him take Sophie on his motorcycle, once without either of them wearing a helmet. That was the last straw."

"Where are your parents? Shouldn't they have supported you?"

"They gave up on me long ago. They didn't want to be parents, let alone grandparents. Both are workaholics who feel their lifework supersedes all else."

Julian snorted. "Bull! Maybe one day they'll see how much they've lost." He got up when Garnet set the album on the bookcase. "Going back to something you said a minute ago…did alcohol change Dale drastically? Did he take Sophie to hurt you because you dumped him? Or was it because he loved her and couldn't stand having nothing but supervised access to her?"

Garnet laced her hands tightly together for a long time. "A secretary at Sophie's preschool said Dale phoned two days later. All he said was 'Tell Garnet we're fine.' He didn't identify himself, but Barb knew his voice. Police had anticipated some contact, but they installed trace equipment on our home phone. There was only that one attempt at communication. Sergeant Savage says we can't be sure it was Dale. There were cranks who wrote me and left messages on my answering machine."

"The fact that he called suggests a guilty conscience, and says something different about him than if he'd never looked back." Julian stepped to the bookcase, opened the album and tilted it toward the light. This time he focused intently on pictures of Garnet's ex.

He could feel her eyes on him, searching for any sign of recognition. When he closed the book at last without comment, he saw her shoulders sag as the last slim hope she'd clung to slipped away. "It's not him, is it?"

There was so much pain in Garnet's flat statement

that Julian quietly took his own photograph from his pocket. Without comment, he passed it to her.

"What's this? Another picture of the little girl. With—a man." She moved closer to the lamp and hunched over the photograph. "You've had this all along? What game are you playing, Detective?"

"No game." Julian's voice was hoarse with emotion. "I have to think of my pop. Can you blame me for being cautious in a matter this potentially explosive?"

Garnet slowly shook her head. "I don't blame you. Heavens, I can't tell from this picture, either. It's better than the other, but still too far away and fuzzy. If it *is* Dale, he's had a makeover. There's his slighter build, and darker, less curly hair. Yet this girl's smile is so like Sophie's my chest aches to see it. I'd give anything just to hug her again." Without warning, Garnet burst into tears and the snapshot fell to the floor.

Julian felt helpless as he retrieved it. Unable to stand by while she fell apart, he did what came naturally. He wrapped Garnet in a tight embrace. Feeling her stiffen, he immediately let go. However, her tears didn't stop, and she kept wiping her cheeks with the heels of her hands.

Saying a silent, *to hell with it,* Julian moved in again, and held her until her tears were spent. "Better?" he murmured against her sweet-smelling hair.

She slid her hands up the front of Julian's shirt and felt the dampness of the cloth from her tears. "Julian…I have to go. To Georgia. Don't you see? I have to. No matter what a plane ticket costs. I'd leave tonight, but I need to arrange time off with my principal first. Please, tell me where to find them. I promise I won't make trouble for your father."

Julian ran his hands up and down her slender back. "I'll change my ticket and fly down with you. You can stay with my folks, which will save you a few bucks. They have a big house with plenty of extra room. Mom complains they rattle around now that the four of us kids are gone."

"I can't barge in on your parents." Leaning back, Garnet shook her head.

"Do it for me," he said, carefully wiping tear stains from beneath her shadowy eyes. "So I know you're safe."

As he spoke, a ripple of awareness passed between them in a totally unguarded moment.

Garnet recognized the feeling for what it was—

interest. A part of her brain said she absolutely should not accept his offer. But what came out of her mouth was far removed from the common sense that normally controlled her. "I accept. It'll be a relief to know someone, uh, anyone, so far from home."

CHAPTER FOUR

JULIAN STEPPED away from Garnet and struggled to understand what he'd just done. What had possessed him to toss out that offer? What right did he have to subject his parents to the ugliness of a domestic kidnapping case?

"Tell me something, Garnet," Julian murmured. "If this guy in Georgia turns out to be your ex, will you call the FBI and have him charged with kidnapping?"

Her sky-blue eyes had begun to clear but now she blinked twice to keep the tears at bay. "Yes. I'm shocked a cop would have to ask that."

"Hear me out. Say it is Dale, but he's become a hard worker with a legitimate job."

"So what?"

Julian rubbed a thumb over the creases in his forehead. "Nothing. You have every right to have him arrested and ask them to throw the book at him."

"I detect a 'but…' in your sudden ramblings." Garnet shrugged off the hand Julian curled gently over her shoulder. Putting some distance between them, she crossed her arms and nervously massaged her elbows.

"I guess my ramblings aren't so sudden." Julian hooked his thumbs through belt loops and paced in a tight circle. "The photo I showed you is too distorted to reflect the love I saw between the man and his daughter. Garnet, I swear there was no friction. Her little face shone the instant she saw him, and when he turned and spotted her in the doorway he… Ah, hell, I can't explain it other than to say his tiredness fell away. I could hear them laughing even from where I stood. The girl flew out of the house into his arms, and he swung her around making airplane sounds."

Reaching for the photo Julian spoke about, Garnet held it under the lamp and she tilted the shade for a better look.

Julian thought perhaps she saw the loving expressions, or the pair's connectedness. But when she spoke, her stuttered query left him no doubt as to the depth of her personal anguish. "If this is S-Sophie—and the resemblance is heartbreaking—

do you honestly think I should let Dale walk f-free? I've spent more than fifteen months living in hell."

She shoved the picture back at Julian. Her lips thinned as she watched him return it to his shirt pocket.

"You have no idea what my pain is like," she said stonily. "Try to imagine, I beg you. Imagine losing someone you love more than life itself. Pile on the agony, the fear you may never see that person again. Maybe my daughter's crying for me every night like I cry for her. I'm supposed to forgive that?" Garnet held out her hands in supplication, then yanked them back and wrapped her arms around her quivering body.

Because she was far from the first parent Julian had ever dealt with who had a missing child, he wasn't immune to her pain. "Shh," he murmured. "I promise it'll be your call." His voice was raspy, and he again reached out to comfort her.

"I hear a 'but' at the end of that sentence, too." Sniffing, she tried not to flatten her nose against his shirtfront as she moved into his arms. But as Julian began slowly massaging away the chill that gripped her, Garnet began to relax.

"No buts, Garnet. I know you're suffering. I've

worked with parents in your situation. It's that I also find myself concerned by how confusing it'll be for the poor girl, should she turn out to be Sophie. I mean, even though the photo's grainy, I believe you do see the love between the girl and her dad. I guess what I'm saying is that I've watched kids' lives be ripped apart in parental scuffles. Eight times out of ten the kid loves Mom and Dad equally. They don't understand, especially at Sophie's age, being yanked from one parent to the other. Garnet, even abused kids love their parents. And the girl I saw in no way seemed abused."

Garnet grew still except for one hand idly bunching the tear-damp fabric over Julian's heart.

He knew he'd given her reason to pause. Reason to think. In his estimation, the fact Garnet was turning things over in her mind said a lot about her. It said she might not go in and snatch the girl back with no regard for the consequences.

In the silence that fell between them, Julian also discovered how much he liked holding Garnet Patton. Another thought followed, throwing a wet blanket over the first—his dad wasn't the only Cavenaugh capable of stepping into trouble up to his neck. Suddenly feeling awkward, Julian untangled himself from Garnet's all-too-inviting arms. "I…ah…didn't intend to make.a pest of myself. I'd better take off."

Garnet nodded, and followed him to the door, though she seemed somewhat confused by his abrupt decision to leave.

"Shall I…uh…try to book a flight to match yours?" She made a feeble gesture toward the phone that sat on her end table. "I wish we could leave tonight. I probably could get hold of my principal. I'm sure he'd understand. But there's no way he could get me a check cut, and I'll need money for my trip. Tuesday is the soonest I can get away."

"Leave booking the flight to me. I'll change my ticket to match yours."

"How will I pay for mine then? I need to use a credit card. I don't know about detectives, but teachers pretty much live paycheck to paycheck."

"We'll work it out." He had the door open and one foot in the hall.

"Wait, how will you get me the details? Shouldn't you take my phone number?"

"Remember, I'm going fishing in the morning with a cop buddy, and I'm bringing Mr. Carlyle my catch. Plus, you and I are going to dinner at

Torinos." That plan held enormous appeal for Julian even though he knew he shouldn't get any more involved.

"Oh, so your friend in Anchorage is a policeman? No wonder you know so much about my case." Garnet bobbed her head as if the odd pieces had finally fallen in place. "Interesting. Tomorrow, you'll have to tell me how you two met. Uh, if it turns out you need anything from me to book the flight, come by the school. We're relaxed once students are gone. I'll just be packing and cleaning up my home room."

"First I need to clear up a misconception. Larry, the friend I'm going fishing with, knows nothing about your case. I'm in this alone. But if he's free, I thought I'd ask him to join us for dinner. If that's all right with you?"

"Certainly. So, is it best if we don't talk about my case tomorrow night? Since you've indicated you're operating outside the law."

"Well, jeez. Put like that, I feel guilty as hell." Gazing at his boots, Julian pinched the bridge of his nose. "Whatever you may think, Garnet, I'm a good cop."

"Please, I didn't mean anything negative. I was

just thinking aloud. If it turns out you've found Sophie, I'll owe you more than I can ever repay."

"That's another thing," he said solemnly, jerking his head up. "I've never wanted to raise your hopes. If it's *not* Sophie, you'll probably hate me forever."

"I'd like to say I'm used to having my heart broken again and again, but each time is just as hard. I do sense you're a caring man. If this turns out to be another disappointment, I promise not to blame you. You're doing your best to protect everyone involved. I'm grateful you didn't flatly refuse to let me tag along. Sergeant Savage would've told me to butt out. He has before."

An amused expression lifted the corners of Julian's mouth. "Don't think I didn't consider it," he admitted, laughing to lessen the sting.

Garnet laughed, too, showing she hadn't lost her sense of humor. "I'd better let you go before Mr. Carlyle hears us and comes out to investigate again. He'd probably grill you over keeping me up so late." She smiled indulgently, but lowered her voice all the same.

"Listen, at the risk of sounding cocky, tell the old guy to plan on salmon. Larry is an avid fisherman. Every time we met at a conference, he bragged about how great the fishing is in Alaska. Now he'll have to put up or shut up."

Garnet smiled again, clearly feeling more relaxed than she'd been earlier.

Overwhelmed by a desire to kiss her, Julian buried both hands in his pockets, twitched his shoulders and all but charged down the stairs. He didn't breathe deeply until he stepped out into cold night air.

Reaching his Jeep, he glanced up, and realized Garnet was framed in her living-room window, gazing down on him. He wondered what she was thinking. Was she wishing he'd stayed longer?

Too far away to see what kind of expression she wore, he lifted a hand and waved. She didn't respond at first, and Julian assumed he'd jumped to conclusions—that she wasn't really looking at him, but maybe checking the weather. Then, just before he slid into the Jeep, Garnet hesitantly raised her right hand.

Julian's pulse jumped. "Damn," he said. "You've got shit for brains, Cavenaugh, getting involved like this." He started the Jeep and roared off before he could reconsider.

Always analytical, he mentally listed a string of

reasons why having amorous feelings for the woman he'd just met was not only bad, but disastrous.

Usually, he heeded his conscience. This time, however, images of Garnet's hopeful eyes stuck with him long after he'd left her.

The images didn't fade even after he took a near frigid shower at his motel, and later buried his head beneath his pillow.

In the morning, he woke up thinking about her, too. All the way to the breakfast café where he was to meet Larry Adams, Julian wrestled with his long-ingrained sense of duty.

"Hey," Larry said the minute Julian climbed down from the Jeep, "you're already beginning to look like a mountain man. It's funny how day-old stubble totally changes your pretty-boy looks. Anybody ever tell you that you'd be great at under-cover work?" Guffawing, Larry clapped Julian's back as he moved them both toward the restaurant.

Julian rubbed his whiskery jaw. "Blast that woman. I never forget to shave."

"What woman?" Larry was clearly intrigued as he slid into a vacant booth and picked up a menu from on the table.

Heaving a sigh, Julian was slower to take his

place on the opposite side. "I wasn't going to involve you, Larry. But the truth is, I wasn't totally up front about my reason for coming to Alaska."

"You really held out, buddy, if you came for a woman." Larry took time out to order pancakes, bacon, eggs and coffee from the waitress who suddenly appeared at the table.

"I'll have the same." Julian let the waitress leave, then he scowled at his friend. "Why do you look so smug? I'm a fellow cop who just admitted lying."

Larry brushed off Julian's concern. "I don't recall you being under oath the day you phoned. You maybe didn't tell me the whole truth, but that's not the same as lying. Supercop that I am, I heard some rumbling at the station yesterday. Enough to figure out it was too coincidental, you showing up here at the same time the lead detective on an old domestic kidnapping case claims some guy's been snooping around town asking questions. Adding two and two together, I guessed it might be you."

Julian gaped at his friend.

The waitress delivered mugs of hot coffee, and both men hoisted their cups. Julian scowled through the curling steam. "I would've told you, but I'm working on a tip. A hunch of my dad's, really. Larry,

I haven't got a single fact. I didn't want your ass in a sling or I'd have asked you to look at the case records."

"I'd have done the same." Then, surprising Julian, Larry said, "Yesterday, on the q.t., I accessed the Patton file. The mom's a real looker. I'm guessing she's the one who has you forgetting to shave… hmm?"

For the first time Julian noticed his friend was clean shaven. When last they'd met, Larry had looked like a street bum. "Hey, did you close your case? You're looking good, and acting cheery so I'm guessing you did. Congratulations!"

"Thanks. So, I guess you didn't see my ugly mug on the morning news. We got lucky and tracked a snitch who led us straight to a boat loaded with tons of cocaine."

Julian toasted Larry's success with a tap of their coffee mugs. "Speaking of boats, instead of stream fishing, I'd like to have a go at catching a salmon. An old guy who lives next door to Mrs. Patton mentioned he can't afford to buy it. He's a nice man, and I'd like to take him some. But I'll understand if you've had enough of boats. I can go solo. I'd already planned to offer you dinner tonight. You and Mrs. Patton. She agreed to join me at a place called Torinos."

"I accept. By the way, Sergeant Gary Savage, the lead in charge of the Patton case, isn't exactly a close friend of mine. I won't be upset at all if you solve this and put his nose out of joint. If you need help, I'm your man."

"Is Savage to blame for letting the case go cold?"

Their stacks of pancakes came, and Larry began to butter his. He reached for the maple syrup before shrugging. "I'm not fond of glory hounds, and Gary is one of the worst. You probably won't hear anyone accusing him of dropping the case the minute the FBI was called in, but if you check the file, I bet you'll find that's what happened."

Julian bit into a piece of crisp bacon. He said nothing until he'd finished the entire slice and washed it down with coffee. "Kidnappings are the fibbies territory."

"Yeah, but it's not even your case and yet here you are."

"Gotcha. If you'd been assigned this one, or I had, we would've fought to stay involved."

Larry wiped his mouth with a paper napkin. "Exactly. The fibs see a thousand grieving moms. A hometown cop ought to take her pain personally.

Feel it in his gut and keep plugging away to solve the case. Know what I'm saying?"

Julian did. Even as Larry talked, Julian pictured Garnet's sad eyes. Her fragility. He had to make a concerted effort to shake off the awareness. "Are we going to sit around all day stuffing ourselves, or are we gonna hit the water and hook a sockeye?"

Swallowing the last bite of his pancake, Larry signaled the waitress for the bill. When she brought it over, he plucked it out of her hand before she set it on the table. "Breakfast is on me," he told Julian. "And since you're planning to give the salmon away," he grumbled, "who cares how tasty it is? Ah!" He stopped shoving the change back in his pocket. "I think I get it. This isn't so much about Mrs. Patton's poor, old neighbor, but with you having developed a thing for the woman herself. Am I right?"

Julian snarled his thanks for breakfast and straight-armed his way out of the restaurant.

Larry followed at a more leisurely pace, laughing all the while. "I've never seen this side of you before. You're always Mr. Eye-On-The-Ball."

"Yeah, well, you're a real pain in the ass, Adams. Garnet Patton happens to be a nice woman to whom life has dealt a low blow." Julian stopped beside his Jeep and threw up his hands. "You of all people know I can't afford to get romantically involved when there's every chance I'm wrong about this. I have no proof the kid my pop stumbled upon *is* Sophie Patton. None! And the grieving mother has pinned all her hopes on me leading her to her daughter." Julian's breath puffed like smoke signals in the crisp morning air. "Quit harassing me. Come on, I'll share everything I know about this case on the way to the marina. Tonight, at dinner, I'd appreciate if you back me up with Garnet. Tell her not to get her hopes too high."

"Hmm." Larry slid into the passenger seat and shoved it back to make room for his longer legs. "Let's hear what you've got first, cowboy." Adams had always teased Julian at conference about his preference for wearing pointy-toed boots.

Julian recounted his side of the story, beginning with the phone call from his mom. He ended after passing Larry the cell phone photos, about the time he parked at the public dock. Pulling on the emergency brake, he added, "She couldn't positively ID the child or the man from those fuzzy pictures. At best, we've got a long shot here."

Larry squinted at the pictures, studying first one then the other. "They *are* crappy pictures." He handed them back and opened his door. "If we hurry, I think we'll still be able to get aboard the *Sockeye Princess.* I believe that's her captain pacing up and down the wharf. He hates going out without a full load of passengers."

Julian sprinted to keep up with his longer-legged pal, who'd guessed right. The captain had, in fact, three openings left on his fishing vessel, and was more than willing to settle for filling two.

"I'll pay the excursion fee, Julian. Will you run across the street to that shack? Rent us each poles, boots and rain slickers."

Glancing up at an azure-blue sky, Julian gaped. "You think it's going to rain?"

"Probably not," the captain said, shoving a smelly, half-smoked cigar into his mouth. "Your buddy's gone out with me before. He knows I go out past the big swells to where the salmon hide. You'll get soaked without boots and slickers." Around his chewed cigar, he added, "Plain you're a cheechako. I hope you aren't one going to upchuck all over my deck, sonny."

"Not me," Julian felt compelled to assure the

leather-skinned grouch. He dashed off to rent the gear and a few minutes later, as he and Larry went aboard, Julian asked quietly, "Larry, what's a chee-chako?"

"A greenhorn. The captain saw those fancy carved snakeskin boots of yours. Up here guys wear manly boots with traction. Out of curiosity, have you ever been deep-sea fishing? I'm asking in case Joe was right about you. I'm gonna fish upwind just to be safe."

"Knock it off. I've fished for marlin out in the gulf plenty of times."

And he had. But the smell of diesel mixed with the rolling chop of Pacific Ocean waves adversely affected several other novices on board.

Either it was sheer determination on his part, or the fact that he was first on deck to hook a fighting silvery fish, but Julian's stomach did fine. The salmon was a beauty, arcing above the waves as it tried to dislodge his hook. The men who weren't too sick all whooped. Larry pounded Julian gleefully on the back. The act of netting his prize successfully rid him of the worries he'd brought to Alaska, and those he'd taken on after meeting Garnet Patton.

Julian let one of the crew take his picture with his

fish. His dad would love a copy, plus it'd ensure bragging rights with his brothers. Julian, Tag and Josh were fiercely competitive and they often swapped fish stories. Proof of fishing prowess kept the jeers to a minimum. Although he supposed his brothers could still accuse him of posing with someone else's catch.

As one of the crew tagged his fish, Julian had the satisfaction of knowing that this time he could enlist Garnet in backing up his story. He thought how great it'd be next week, to have someone in his corner, since Josh and Tag's wives always jumped into family fish arguments on their behalf.

All in all, six salmon were caught before Captain Joe turned the *Sockeye Princess* back into Cook Inlet. Of the six, Julian's fish was biggest. Larry didn't hook a single one.

"I hope your girlfriend's neighbor has a big appetite," Larry said when they turned in their gear, then bought a foam cooler that was almost too small for Julian's fish.

"She's not my girl," Julian said, straightening from loading the cooler in the back of his Jeep. "If you keep talking like that, Larry, you'll be uninvited for dinner tonight. Reservations are for six o'clock, by the way."

"Well, I'm not the one taking the lady home to meet dear old Mom and Dad."

Julian flooded the Jeep's engine. "Dammit, Larry, my pop's the reason I'm up here. Granted, I ought to put Garnet up in a hotel. But if she's stuck in some hotel with time on her hands, she'll be more likely to charge over to the guy's house and accuse him of stealing her daughter."

"Yeah, that would be bad. If she's wrong, she could end up in jail for making false charges. If she's right, the ex could do her in and take off with the kid."

"That's exactly what I told Garnet. She needs to take this slow."

"Damn, I hate domestic squabbles, don't you?"

Julian nodded glumly. "What I dislike most is how the kids always get screwed."

"Any chance of Garnet and her ex kissing and making up?"

Blindsided by Larry's off-hand remark, Julian realized he didn't want to think about that possibility. Not that it was one. He couldn't imagine Garnet wanting to reconcile with the man who'd stolen her daughter. And besides, there was a new woman in the mix, too.

"Man, don't scowl at me like that. You know as well as I do that women in domestic cases can and do act damned unpredictable."

"Sorry," Julian said, pulling in next to Larry's pickup outside the café where they'd had breakfast. "I was just wishing my pop was a plumber, a fry cook or anything but a mailman who delivers hundreds of those lost-kid cards each year."

Larry dug in his front pocket for his keys. "I hear you, buddy. But looking at this objectively, your dad's pretty special. Out of millions of mail carriers, how many do you suppose bother to give those cards a second look? If more were as conscientious as your dad, maybe more cases would be solved."

Looping his arms around his steering wheel, Julian set his chin on his hands and eyed his friend, who now glared in through the open driver's-side window.

"Yeah, Pop's a good man. You're probably one of the few who understands how messy this could get, and why I started out hoping against hope that Pop was wrong. Then I met Garnet, and…" Julian closed his eyes and didn't finish his sentence.

Larry smacked his hands twice on the door sill. "I can't wait to meet this paragon who's torturing you like this. Six, you said? Is the reservation in your name?"

"Yes. And speaking of reservations, I need to get back to my motel and call the airline to book Garnet a flight and/or juggle mine."

Cocking both fingers like pistols, Larry stepped away from the Jeep. "Say, that reminds me. Here's the number of the picture of you and your fish. They'll be displayed on sandwich boards this evening outside the shack where you rented our gear. Costs ten bucks a copy," he said, passing Julian a business card. "Not bad for a genuine Alaskan souvenir. You might want to pick up a couple on your way to dinner."

That snapped Julian out of his funk. He was in Alaska, a spot he'd dreamed of visiting since he was a boy and saw a documentary on salmon fishing. Now he'd fished those straits, and had caught a fine sockeye. He pocketed the business card and made a mental note to collect the photos that would give proof to his adventure.

THREE HOURS LATER, after he'd added ice to the cooler, and had showered off the smell of fish and the captain's cigar, Julian stood at the front door to

Garnet's building. He balanced the cooler on a hip as he pressed the buzzer.

The speaker crackled and her voice interrupted his study of a fantastic sunset. He'd never envisioned an Alaskan sky strafed purple, pink and molten red. When he finally arrived at Garnet's apartment, she held the door open for him as he struggled to carry the heavy cooler.

"Wow, no wonder you took so long to climb the stairs. Mr. Carlyle just got home from the park. He'll be so pleased."

Julian set down the cooler, letting Garnet roust her neighbor.

"Actually, I was admiring the sunset." He gestured expressively with both hands. "I felt like I was in an IMAX presentation. Just me and all that color."

She smiled as John Carlyle and Hoover joined them. "Everything's bigger in Alaska, haven't you heard?" Garnet said, even as John inspected the salmon and exclaimed, "Mercy, that's certainly true of this fish. Son, you have enough fish here to feed everyone in the building."

"Julian, maybe we should stay and help John and Hoover host a salmon feed. I can cook salmon steaks on the barbecue in our courtyard."

"I guess I could cancel the reservations and call Larry to let him know the plan's changed, if that's what you want."

Mr. Carlyle set the lid back on the cooler. "No, no. You youngsters run on along and have a good time. I'll get Anna Winkleman to help. As long as Hoover and I get two helpings each of salmon." He patted Julian's shoulder. "Can't thank you enough for this treat."

"You're quite welcome. I wouldn't have gone salmon fishing if it hadn't been for you. On our way to dinner, Garnet, I need to swing by and get some copies of the photo the crew chief took of me on the boat with my catch. My two brothers will be so envious."

Garnet smiled indulgently. "Did they hang the fish on the scale that shows how long it is? Otherwise, before you carry it down to the patio for John, I could go get my sewing tape."

"The captain marked the length, but thanks. A crew member took pictures, too. I'll swing by the marina on our way to the restaurant and pick them up. I *am* counting on you to back me up, though, when my brothers try to say I didn't catch this baby."

"Oh, then you scheduled my flight?"

"I did. We leave Tuesday at one-twenty."

"Good. That's good. John, shall I ask Anna to start notifying residents of your salmon feed, while you show Julian to the community kitchen?"

The beaming old man nodded.

Hoisting the cooler to his shoulder, Julian followed him to the elevator. Halfway down to the room off the basement patio it dawned on him that Garnet had engineered it so he'd help John without making it obvious. Her kindness touched him. It reminded him of something his mom would do. He was more convinced than ever that Garnet would fit well in his parents' home in Mosswood. She wasn't a Southerner, but all the same she practiced Southern hospitality.

"John, I have time to help you cut salmon steaks if you'd like," Julian said.

"I'd appreciate it. I'm not as steady with a knife as I used to be. You're a good man, son. I must remember to tell Anna Winkleman how thoughtful you are. She and others in the building are worried about Garnet traipsing off down south with you. I'll let them know there's no need to fret."

"Thanks for the vote of confidence." Julian accepted the knife the old man pulled from one of the drawers, and began cutting one-inch steaks.

"Garnet's more upbeat than I've seen her since she moved here. She's had a lot of disappointments. Is this gonna be another?"

Julian stopped cutting. "I wish I knew. I told her she shouldn't get her hopes up. But she has, and I'm worried about her. That's the biggest reason why I want her to stay with my folks. They're good, caring people. If this child isn't Sophie, I'm hoping my mother can help Garnet through what will surely be a bad time."

John Carlyle studied Julian for several seconds before nodding. "Yep, you're okay. Our Garnet's gonna be in good hands."

Julian dipped his head and kept cutting the salmon steaks. He finished about the time Anna Winkleman arrived carrying a sack of rice and a big bowl filled with salad.

Excusing himself, Julian bounded up the stairs to Garnet's apartment, assuring himself at the landing that John's confidence in him wasn't misplaced.

CHAPTER FIVE

JULIAN TAPPED on Garnet's door.

"It's open," she called.

He entered the apartment and found Garnet by the sofa, surrounded by piles of clothes and toiletries. He raised one eyebrow quizically.

"I'm packing," Garnet explained. "I thought I'd take enough for two weeks. It's probably just a matter of me identifying if it's Sophie, then the FBI will let me bring her home." She stood over an open suitcase, looking anxious and clutching a long-sleeve blouse to her midriff with both hands.

Julian's eyes zeroed in on a medium-size brown teddy bear in one corner of the suitcase. The bear's matted fur told him it had been well hugged. "Damn, Garnet! You're asking to get your heart broken in little pieces again." Running one hand through his hair, he gestured to the stuffed toy with the other.

"Bear-bear was Sophie's favorite toy. She carted

him everywhere. Dale left him at her preschool."
Bending, Garnet caressed the furry ears, then tucked
the bear carefully under a stack of clothing. Her lips
trembled, but she pressed them together tightly and
began folding the blouse.

Julian turned away from the scene. He swallowed
hard but he couldn't speak. He'd tried to warn Garnet
against pinning all her expectations on his father's
hunch. She'd done it anyway. Chances were his dad
was wrong. If that happened, Julian would always be
haunted by a shattered woman and that damn bear.

Without looking at her, he said, "You won't want
long sleeves this time of year in Georgia. Even if it
rains, it'll likely be steamy hot."

"I appreciate your concern, but I don't have
anything else. I'll have to roll up my sleeves. If this
turns out to be the lead I've prayed for, my comfort
will be immaterial. I'd walk barefoot through hot
coals to bring Sophie home."

He spun back to her. "I know that, Garnet. It's
what concerns me most."

She added a second blouse to the suitcase. "The
last time Sergeant Savage phoned me to say he'd
received any kind of tip was Christmas Eve. I'm
sure you're aware that the holidays bring all the

nutcase crank callers out of their slimy holes. Even interviewing someone twisted and perverted was better than these last five empty months. A long shot is better than no shot."

"I'll buy that." He checked his watch. "It's almost six. We should get going. We don't want Larry to send out the canine patrol."

"You said you needed to pick up the pictures of you with your fish and I'd like to finish packing. There's not much left, but there's no sense tying you up. Why don't you go on ahead and have drinks with your friend. I'll join you for dinner by, say, six-thirty?"

"You planning to stand us up, Garnet?"

"No. Why would I?"

"Oh, I don't know. If you're hungry, there's a salmon feed downstairs. It also crossed my mind that maybe you plan to catch the red-eye to Denver tonight, and transfer on to Atlanta in order to beat me there and speed things up to suit yourself."

She looked surprised, then hurt. "And do what, Julian? I don't even know where your parents live. You don't trust me enough to even tell me the name of their town! What have I done to deserve that?"

Julian reached for the doorknob. "Sorry, hazards

of the job. Veteran cops don't trust anyone. My parents are Samuel and Beth Cavenaugh. They live in Mosswood, Georgia." He strode to the door, went out and closed it solidly.

Garnet's mouth fell open. He hadn't added that he'd see her at Torinos at six-thirty. The jerk really expected her to stand him up and take that midnight flight out of Anchorage. Which meant she would've deliberately planned to stick him with the cost of the ticket he'd bought for her for Tuesday. What kind of women did Julian Cavenaugh usually associate with, for heaven's sake?

She stomped around, throwing things in her suitcase until she had to sit on the lid to close it. The clock ticked steadily until it was time to leave for Torinos. She was still wearing her work clothes. And because the principal had okayed her early leave, she'd raced around like a crazy woman, packing everything she thought she'd need. She could definitely use a shower. However, it'd serve Julian right if she showed up smelling less than appealing.

Ugh, she wouldn't do that to his friend.

Garnet flipped on the light in her small bathroom and turned both faucets. Let him stew a while. Let him picture her on her way to the airport. She intended to shower off the day's grime and put on something that would knock his eyes out.

Did she even own such an item? She wasn't generally one for playing the femme fatale. So maybe knocking his eyes out was a stretch.

She did have a peach angora dress with a portrait collar that Jenny had coerced her into buying for the teachers' winter potluck. It hit her about four inches above the knee. She'd worn tights at the potluck. Tonight, she dried off and slipped into the dress without covering her clean-shaven legs.

At the mirror, she slicked on lip gloss and as she blotted her lips, she donned her only good pair of earrings. Her grandmother's Australian fire opals.

It was six-thirty on the dot when she unlocked her car. With any luck, she'd walk into Torinos no more than fifteen minutes late. But late enough to make Julian sweat.

JULIAN SAT FACING the restaurant door. His cell phone was on the table, but the low lighting and the flickering candle made it difficult to keep track of the time. Twice he'd waved off the waiter.

Larry broke off in the middle of a sentence. "Pick

up the damn phone and call the lady. If she can't get here on time, I say to hell with her. We rushed through breakfast and skipped lunch. I'm hungry enough to eat a bear."

"So, we'll order," Julian said, pocketing his phone without a glance as he signaled the hovering waiter. "Garnet said she'd be here by six-thirty and it's past that." He snatched up one of the menus he'd set aside.

The front door swung open, letting the noise of the street into the restaurant. Julian glanced over his menu. His jaw dropped when he spotted Garnet speaking with the maitre d'. Was that Garnet? He squinted for a better look.

Their waiter, a man of some bulk, cut off Julian's view. He craned his neck to see around the portly fellow.

"Sir! I asked if you gentlemen are ready to order. I understood you expected a lady to join you."

"We did. Do. Are." Leaping to his feet, Julian left his gaping pal and the flustered waiter, and made his way to the door to greet Garnet.

"Ah, here's my friend now," she told the maitre d'. "Sorry, Julian, I didn't see you when I first came in. I hope I'm not too, too late," she said. "It took longer to get ready than I anticipated."

She was so beautiful, yet so falsely contrite, Julian was torn between wanting to kiss her or call her bluff. Curbing both urges, he placed a hand on her back and let it slide down the soft fabric of her dress to her waist. "Are you late?" he asked mildly. "I hadn't noticed. Larry and I were busy catching up."

The flash of his dark eyes told quite a different story. Garnet mentally awarded herself one point. Although, they shouldn't be adversaries. She had to trust him. And as much as she suspected that he'd offered her a room with his family in order to keep her on a short leash in Georgia, it could all just be in her mind.

Her motherly instincts were saying the child in his photos was her baby, her Sophie. Garnet wouldn't be deterred from following this lead. By herself, if necessary.

Julian stopped beside a table midway into the room. "Larry, I'd like you to meet Garnet Patton. Garnet, Larry Adams is the friend I mentioned earlier."

Larry, who was in the process of ordering spaghetti with meat-and-mushroom sauce, shut his gaping mouth and stood. His napkin dropped to the floor, and he stumbled all over his feet rushing to pull out Garnet's chair.

"Why, thank you," she said sweetly, barely managing to resist an impulse to tug her skirt down as she sat.

The men's eyes clashed and their shoulders bumped as they both tried to scoot Garnet's chair closer to the table. If she'd been looking at them, she would've been amused by their male posturing.

Larry handed her a menu with a flourish, and told the waiter to give her a few minutes to look over the selections.

Julian couldn't hold his tongue. "What happened to not waiting a minute longer to order, and being hungry as a bear?" he snapped.

"Are you familiar with the menu?" Larry asked Garnet, flatly ignoring Julian. But it was too much for Julian to overlook when Larry braced his arm on the back of Garnet's chair and gave her a rundown on several items, such as the cannelloni and rigatoni.

"Garnet lives nearby," Julian drawled. "She and her colleagues come here a lot."

"Oh." Larry pulled back.

"That's okay," Garnet said sweetly. "I didn't realize everything that went into cannelloni. Maybe

I'll have that. I tend to stick with the same old boring lasagne."

Disgusted at how she and Larry were all but snuggling in front of him, Julian briskly motioned the waiter again. As the server started in their direction, Julian noticed a big man with a craggy face and a gray crew cut also striding toward their table. The guy had "cop" written all over him. Suddenly, Julian pictured himself being interrogated down at the Anchorage precinct. He'd probably get the book thrown at him for meddling in an open case and rightly so. He knew better. Chief MacHale would vouch for him, but he wouldn't be happy about it, and Julian would catch hell when he got back to Atlanta.

Larry wasn't paying attention to anyone except Garnet, so Julian kicked him under the table, alerting him to trouble, but too late. The steel-haired man stopped next to Larry's chair and barked, "Adams, I thought it was you sitting here with Mrs. Patton." Hard gray eyes swept over Julian. "I don't believe I've met your friend. New in town or just passing through?" he asked abruptly.

Garnet whirled at the sound of the man's voice. "Sergeant Savage. How…uh…nice to see you."

Larry leaned back in his chair. "We're celebrating my big drug bust, Gary. I trust you heard about it at the station. What's your reason for coming here? Have you finally put the lid on one of your missing-person cases?"

Julian didn't miss the dark red flush that spread across the sergeant's jowls.

"It's my wife's birthday," Savage snapped. "I'm still waiting for an introduction to your pal. Or should I say your partner in crime?"

"My cousin?" Larry asked without missing a beat. The problem was he said it at the same time as Julian rose from his chair, extended a hand and announced, "I'm a shirttail relative of Larry's mom. I came up here to do a little fishing. Caught a salmon today. A beauty."

Savage didn't shake Julian's proffered hand. Instead, he narrowed his eyes at Larry. "I wouldn't call a cousin a *distant* relative. And none of that explains how you happen to be dining with a principal from one of my cases. A case that some guy impersonating a cop or a reporter has been poking into for days."

Feeling the tension mount at the table, Garnet made a show of checking her watch. "If you men are going to talk business, I'll excuse myself and go call Jenny. I can't imagine what's keeping her."

Setting her napkin on her plate, she nudged Julian as she bent and dug a cell phone out of her purse. Rising, she angled herself between their table and Gary Savage, forcing him to step back. "The saying, 'it's a small world' is so true," she said, aiming her comment at the sergeant. "Larry's second cousin is a childhood friend of my colleague, Jenny Hoffman. It's so like her to invite me to double-date and then forget to come. Do you want to call her, Julian, or shall I?" She nipped at her upper lip, looking genuinely perplexed.

Julian and Larry were so flabbergasted by how cleverly Garnet extricated them from the mess they'd blundered into, they almost missed picking up on her cue. But Julian did eventually react. "Uh, you can call her. The other day was the first time I've seen her since we were kids."

The waiter barged in, pad and pencil at the ready. "You'll order now for yourselves and the lady, no?"

"No," the two men said in unison. "Bring us another round of beer," Larry instructed.

"And the lady will take a Cosmopolitan," Julian added. He hoped Garnet liked the drink he'd seen on her table the other night at the lounge. Although, she'd traded it for coffee, he recalled.

Gary Savage seemed to have been neatly cut from the exchange. He glared at both men and straightened his tie. "Adams, if I find out you're the one who's been sticking your nose in Mrs. Patton's case, your ass is grass." Spinning on a heel, he stomped back to where he'd left a woman, presumably his wife, seated alone in a booth on the other side of the room.

"Phew," Julian muttered. "Close call, that."

"Bad luck, you mean, choosing the same restaurant Savage picked to celebrate his wife's birthday." Larry snatched up his menu. "Darn, I wasn't lying about being starved. Now we have to wait for another chick to show up? I hope you know Gary's not going to take his eyes off us until he finishes his meal. Do you think Garnet can convince her friend to meet us on such short notice?"

"I don't know. Probably." Julian remembered how eager Jenny had been to have him meet her at the teachers' happy hour the day he questioned her outside the high school. "Listen, Larry, we only need to act chummy with Jenny for a few hours. In three days, Garnet and I are flying to Atlanta. Out of Savage's reach."

"You've met Jenny?"

Julian nodded.

"Wow, buddy, you get around. I live here and can't seem to meet any interesting women. You've been here, what, a couple of days and have a slew of them?"

"Two isn't a slew. I've met maybe three at Garnet's school. Teachers. When school starts again you ought to volunteer to speak about saying no to drugs at one of their assemblies or something."

"No, thanks. I did that a couple of years ago. I parked my squad car right out front of the building. When my partner and I came out, our car was jacked up and all four of our tires had been stolen. Worse, we never found the culprits."

Julian nearly spewed his beer all over the table he laughed so hard. He sobered up when he saw that Gary Savage was indeed keeping an eye on them, and that their waiter was growing pretty exasperated with their antics, as well.

IN THE LADIES' ROOM, Garnet paced as she talked to Jenny. "Please, just do me this one huge favor. You hinted every way from Sunday that you wanted Julian to show up at our happy hour yesterday. I know this is really short notice, but hey, it's a free meal. And you love Italian food. Please! His friend?

I guess he's nice looking. But, Jenny, this isn't a real date. You're supposed to have known Julian when you were kids. I know I shouldn't lie. I did it so Gary Savage couldn't get Julian and Larry in trouble. You said yourself Gary's too arrogant to want to share a case. Bottom line, Jenny…none of this is about me, or you or the guys. It's about maybe finding Sophie after all this time."

She stopped pacing and bobbed her head. "I knew I could count on you, Jen. Wear? Whatever gets you here quickest. I'll order you a drink. Long Island iced tea okay?" Garnet closed her phone, took a deep breath and hurried back to the table.

"Okay, guys, she's on her way. Oh, who ordered me a Cosmo? Thanks. We'll need to order Jenny a Long Island iced tea."

Larry touched his beer bottle to Garnet's glass. "Here's to your quick thinking. If it had been up to me and Julian, we'd have put both feet in our mouths for sure."

Julian got the waiter's attention once again. The man hustled over to the table. "You're ready to order?" he inquired, not even trying to disguise a sigh as he pulled out his notepad.

"Actually," Julian said, "we have another person

on the way. We just need to order her beverage. Garnet, you didn't happen to ask what Jenny would like to eat?"

"Sorry, no." She looked doubly guilty about it when Larry's stomach growled loudly enough so even the people at the next table glanced their way.

Julian opened his menu. "Tell you what, we'll have a round of appetizers. Fried cheese with marinara sauce, the artichoke dip and bread sticks. That should do for starters, and take the edge off Larry's hunger."

"Make it a double order of fried cheese," Larry put in.

Satisfied, the waiter trundled off toward the kitchen.

A sparkling Jenny Hoffman sashayed up to the table two minutes after the appetizers arrived. She wore a black T-shirt with a sequined panther on the prowl, black jeans that hugged her long legs and boots that added three inches to her height. Julian hadn't recalled her being this hot the first time they'd met. He belatedly managed to get out of his seat and kiss her cheek before he introduced her to Larry.

"Oh, those appetizers look delicious," she gushed, sitting down and diving right in. "Pleased to meet you, Larry. And thanks, everyone, for letting me horn in on your private outing," she said.

The charm bracelet she wore on her right arm tinkled musically as Jenny helped herself to dip and bread sticks.

Even though inviting Jenny had been her idea, Garnet was unprepared for the stab of jealousy when Julian stood and greeted the latecomer.

And that annoyed her. Hadn't she learned her lesson the last time she fell hard and fast for a man she barely knew? Dale had changed. How could she be sure that Julian Cavenaugh was the kind and compassionate man he appeared to be? He'd lied to get her friends to open up. He'd been quick to invent a story to throw Gary off track. Well, she'd participated, too, but Julian seemed a chameleon. Hadn't he insinuated the other night that maybe she shouldn't prosecute Dale? Perhaps it was true what she'd heard said about good old boys from the South banding together against women. She'd hate to think of Julian being like that. But what did she really know about him?

The waiter seemed relieved to have a full table at last and came over eagerly to take their orders.

"Ladies first," Larry said. "I've warded off my

hunger with appetizers, so I can afford to be magnanimous."

Jenny had no trouble making up her mind. "Spaghetti with meat-and-mushroom sauce," she said. "With a Caesar salad on the side."

"A woman after my own heart," Larry said, beaming at her. "That's exactly what I ordered when Julian and I thought there was only going to be two of us eating."

The waiter quickly circled the table taking orders. "Anything else?"

"Yes." Larry spoke up. "Send a bottle of champagne to the couple in the booth directly across the room from us, with our compliments to the lady on her birthday."

The waiter gave Larry a choice of three kinds of champagne. He settled on a medium priced one.

"Why would you do that?" Julian protested. "That's like thumbing your nose at Savage."

"Actually, I consider it more insurance that he won't come over again and try to make a big stink. He hadn't ordered any champagne. I predict his wife will be so pleased the old boy won't be able to do anything but send us his thanks."

"Hmm. You may be right. I just don't want to

draw his attention before Garnet and I can get out of town."

Jenny set down her drink and leaned toward Julian. "How sure are you that the little girl you're taking Garnet to see is Sophie?"

Frowning faintly, Julian said, "I'm not sure of anything. I never suggested I had anything to offer but my father's hunch. I've been honest about that, haven't I, Garnet?"

Startled to hear her name, she glanced up from where she'd been fiddling with her napkin. "You sound as if you hope it won't be Sophie."

"Not at all." His words rang hollow even to him, and he glanced away. "That's not entirely true. For your sake, I hope it's her. But I won't lie—I'd rather not have my dad mixed up in this."

"You don't want him to be a hero?" Jenny seemed surprised.

"If he's right," Julian muttered, and was thankful to see the waiter returning with their salads. The arrival of their meals gave him the opportunity to steer the conversation in another direction. Particularly when the waiter delivered a note to Larry with Gary Savage's curt thanks for the champagne.

Smirking, Larry pocketed the note. He turned his

attention to his meal and made small talk with Jenny, who sat across from him. They quickly discovered they had several things in common, and halfway through the meal talked of getting together again.

Julian listened to their animated discussion about hiking trails. He had little to add, but he suddenly realized Garnet hadn't said a word since their food came. He watched for several minutes. "You're awfully quiet," he finally said. "Are you not a big outdoor person?"

Her eyes flew up. "I'm sorry, what? I'm afraid my mind drifted. I wondered…well, I forgot to ask what time we arrive in Atlanta."

"We have a two-and-a-half-hour layover in Minneapolis. It was the best I could do on short notice. With time changes and everything, we land in Atlanta a little after 9:00 p.m. I hope you don't mind, but I took the liberty of asking my parents to meet us at the airport. It's a good way for you all to get to know each other on the drive to Mosswood."

"So, will it be too late to swing by the girl's house?"

Julian noticed she was pushing her cannelloni around on her plate, but she probably hadn't eaten a bite. The fried cheese he'd urged on her earlier lay untouched on her bread plate.

"Garnet, relax and try to let the chips fall where they may. Please eat something or you won't have the stamina to face whatever we find in Georgia."

"That's easy for you to say."

"Surprisingly, it's not." Julian hadn't intended to admit to being nervous, and he was glad Larry and Jenny had their heads together laughing and weren't paying attention.

"I'm afraid my stomach is too jumpy for this rich food," Garnet said. "Would you be terribly upset if I had it boxed to take home to Hoover?"

Julian curled his hand over hers. "If you want to leave, I'll have them pack mine to take back to my motel, too. I'll see if they can find me a plastic fork to go with it."

Larry heard that exchange. "No sneaking off, you two. Garnet, you're the one who let Sergeant Savage think we were double-dating. He probably expects us to head to a movie or a lounge after we finish here. So, unless you want him to get suspicious enough to start running background checks on Julian, we'd better plan something."

"All right," Garnet reluctantly agreed.

Julian was ready to call it a night, but he had to admit Larry had a point.

"How should we play it, then?" Julian asked as he picked up the tab for the entire bill over mild protestations from Larry and louder ones from Garnet. "Stop," he admonished them. "This was my idea. Anyway, since we all came in separate cars, I think all we need to do is walk out of here together. And Garnet, I forgot to say I'll pick you up around ten on Tuesday. I need time to turn in my rental at the airport. It makes no sense for you to pay what it'll cost for long-term parking."

"How long will that be?" Jenny asked, adjusting the strap of her purse over her shoulder as they all stood. "Did you book a return flight?"

"I'm thinking no more than two weeks," Garnet supplied.

Julian shook his head. "There's no telling what will be involved in reclaiming custody should the girl turn out to be Sophie. I left your return ticket open-ended."

The seriousness of her friend's journey seemed to sink in for Jenny. She said earnestly, "Garnet, keep me in the loop, okay? I'm going to burn good-luck candles the whole time you're gone. And if you e-mail me your flight information, I'll pick you up when you return. You, and hopefully Sophie."

Tears flooded her eyes as Garnet thanked Jenny with a hug.

Julian, though, didn't want to think about Garnet leaving Atlanta when they hadn't even gotten there yet.

Larry herded their group toward the door. "You all sure know how to toss a wet blanket on a party. I suggest we walk off our dinner by going to the Silver Springs Lounge for a nightcap. If Savage is as nosy as I'm betting he is, he'll make an excuse to his wife and follow us outside at a discreet distance. He'll see us walking down the street together, and maybe it will put his curiosity to rest long enough for you two to get out of Alaska."

Julian knew Garnet would prefer to climb into her car and go straight home. Not wishing to cause her any added stress, he deferred to her.

"Maybe a cognac will help me sleep. I'll go, but let me drop this box of leftovers off in my car first," she said.

Julian took her arm. "Larry, you and Jenny head on out. I'll walk Garnet to her car and we won't be far behind you."

Garnet had just locked her car again, and they'd quickened their steps to catch up to the others when

Julian grabbed her hand and squeezed it in warning. "Don't look now, but Larry got it right. Your friend the sergeant has just stepped out of the restaurant. He's lighting up, pretending to grab a smoke. I'll lay odds he's really checking on us."

"Why? He was so helpful and attentive in the beginning. I know his calls have tapered off, but I assumed he was still actively working on my case. He said the leads just stopped coming in."

"They probably did, Garnet. I have nothing against Savage personally. If we find Sophie, we'll bring him into the loop."

"Jenny thinks he dropped the ball. It sounded as if Larry thought so, too."

"He hasn't shelved your case totally, or else he wouldn't be trying to find out who I am and why someone's interviewing old witnesses. It's not complicated, Garnet. He's wondering if he missed anything important. I feel bad, because he probably hasn't. I just don't feel bad enough to come clean with him and run the risk of getting my butt kicked by my boss. He has no idea I'm here doing anything but fishing."

"All right, then. Let's go have that cognac. I meant to ask, before you saw Gary and we got off talking about him. Do you think Larry seems interested in Jenny? Romantically, I mean?"

"I don't know." Julian took Garnet's arm as they crossed the street.

"He's not married or with anyone is he?"

"He got burned not long after he got out of the academy, and he's divorced. Are you sure you're asking for Jenny and not yourself? You two were pretty cozy over the menu back there."

She sloughed off his concern, giving him a well-placed elbow in the ribs. "Jenny comes from money. She broke away from her family, but she still dates blue-collar guys she knows aren't acceptable to her folks. They're nice men who fall head over heels for her. Then she develops a boatload of guilt and dumps the poor guy. What's Larry's background? If he's not old money, you may want to warn him to go slow."

"I don't know that much about him. We hung out together at a few police conferences. We were both domestic violence reps from our respective departments. He's transferred to narcotics, and I went to homicide. All beside the point. Why interfere? Why not let them work everything out?"

"I guess you're right. Who listens to anyone else when it comes to relationships?"

"Yeah," he drawled, wondering if that applied to the prickles of interest he was feeling for the woman next to him. He opened the door to the lounge and ushered her into the dark, smoky interior. A bluesy saxophone wailed from a small stage off to one side. A waitress in a skimpy skirt and stiletto heels said she'd just served their friends. She pointed to a corner where Larry and Jenny sat with their heads together. "I see them, thanks." Julian passed the woman a folded bill. "My date and I will join them for a drink. Could we get two Hennessys, please?"

The waitress was back with their drinks almost before Julian wove through the gyrating bodies packed together on a postage-stamp-size dance floor.

"Keep the change," he said, pulling up chairs for himself and Garnet.

They listened to a couple of songs, but it wasn't long before he noticed her rubbing her temples. The music, especially the drums, had grown louder. Leaning over, Julian tapped Larry's shoulder. "Hey, buddy, Garnet and I are gonna take off. She needs some downtime. I'll touch base with you on Monday. By the way, thanks for today. The fishing was great. I have the pictures to brag to my brothers."

Julian passed Larry his business card, leaned in and whispered, "If you get a look at Garnet's case file and see anything interesting, e-mail me."

Larry stood. The friends shook hands. "Take care." Larry leaned nearer Julian. "Thanks for introducing me to Jenny. It's been a while since I've met a woman I've liked this much. And she's agreed to a date next weekend." Larry slapped Julian heartily on the back. Julian considered passing on Garnet's warning, but ended up just wishing Larry well.

Julian escorted Garnet to her car. "If you wait for me to drive around, I'll see you home." He'd parked the Jeep in a lot behind the restaurant.

"There's no need. Thanks for dinner. I'll be in the lobby at ten next Tuesday when you come to pick me up." She shut her door and started the engine.

He watched her merge with the traffic, and reminded himself that she was a big girl. This was, after all, her town. Still, he stood at the curb until she rounded the corner and drove out of sight.

CHAPTER SIX

IT TOOK JULIAN less than an hour Tuesday morning to shower, shave and pack. Afterward, he phoned home. "Mom, glad I caught you. I wanted to make sure you have our flight arrival time. I left details on your answering machine over the weekend."

"We got your message and we'll be at the airport when you arrive. Your dad's more certain than ever that he's right about the girl, and he can't wait to meet Ms. Patton."

"Then you are okay with letting Garnet stay with you until this is settled?"

"Oh, Julian, that poor woman. I can't even imagine all she's gone through. You know we'll do our level best to make her welcome. Personally, I'd like to have this over and done with. I'm sure you feel the same. But, goodness, I also can't help thinking how awful it will be for her if this turns out *not* to be her child."

"I don't think she's even considering that right

now. She claims I brought her the first lead she's had in months. I hope it *is* a lead."

"I hope so, too, for her sake and Sam's. Have a good flight, dear. We'll see you tonight." They hung up, and Julian spent some time just sitting there—hoping he was doing the right thing by taking Garnet to Georgia. Now that he'd gotten to know her better, he really did want the little girl in Mosswood to be her child. But, right or wrong, his pop would bear the brunt either way. So, which was better—wishing his dad had never seen the girl, in which case Julian never would have met Garnet, or praying the child was Sophie Patton? Then they'd all end up dealing with the FBI and the media, and his family would be in the spotlight once again.

He decided that finding Sophie for Garnet beat everything else, hands down. And maybe they could keep things low-key.

Still having time on his hands, Julian crossed to the twenty-four-hour restaurant opposite his motel and ordered breakfast. By the time he paid his bill and settled his account at the motel, it was time to go pick up Garnet.

She must've been watching for him, because she

emerged from her building pulling a medium-size suitcase and carrying a tote over one shoulder.

Julian recognized Anna Winkleman, John Carlyle and his terrier—and was that the crotchety Miss Webber among those swarming around Garnet, hugging her?

As Garnet disengaged from her friends and started toward the Jeep, Julian saw she wore a cream-colored T-shirt and fitted black jeans for travel. Her blond hair hung loose and flew like spun gold threads in the morning breeze. She made as pretty a picture as Julian had ever seen. His heart beat a bit faster.

Leaving the Jeep, he rushed to take her bags.

She handed them over, then turned and waved to the seniors still huddled at the door. Julian waved, too. "Garnet, you mentioned missing having parents who cared about you. Well, those three certainly do. They're your surrogate family," he said, smiling down at her as he fit her suitcase next to his in the space behind the seats.

"They are, aren't they? I never thought about it like that before. I can tell they're worried for me. But I'm just anxious to see if you've found Sophie."

"Not me. If there's any credit due, it belongs to

my pop." Julian held the passenger door open for her, then went around to the driver's side.

"You still have reservations, don't you?" she asked as they pulled away from the curb.

"Yes, but I can't see any other way to do this without calling the FBI and having them question this guy," he said.

"Out of curiosity, why don't you want to do that?"

"Two reasons. It's the same office who sent agents the last time Pop phoned the National Center for Missing and Exploited Children's hot line. Even if the agents have changed, they'll still have a record in their files. And if this guy's not your ex, his neighbors won't forget he was a suspect in a domestic kidnapping. Mosswood is a typical small town. Rumors, gossip—all that can get out of hand fast. It's really easy to ruin someone's reputation. That's just the way it is."

Garnet folded her hands in her lap. "I would hate to cause an innocent person grief. But I'll do whatever it takes to get Sophie back, Julian."

"I'm aware of that. And that possibility, slim though it may be, is the reason I came to Alaska. It's why I stuck my nose in a case I'm not assigned to, and why I'm taking you to Georgia with me."

An uneasy silence hung between them as Julian navigated through traffic to the airport parking lot where he needed to return the Jeep. He unloaded their suitcases, then completed his transaction at the booth.

"I'll take my bags," Garnet said as Julian started to gather his duffel and her two suitcases.

He didn't answer, but his look told her to let him be a gentleman.

"Is there anything you want out of your tote for the flight?" he asked. He was fiddling with the handle of his duffel bag as they approached the ticket counter. He supposed nerves had made him antsy. "Otherwise I'll check everything through to Atlanta," he said, stepping in line.

"My purse is all I need."

"No book or fashion magazine to read on the plane?" He removed his laptop and a battered copy of David Baldacci's book *The Collectors* from his duffel before he rezipped it and set it on the conveyor belt.

Garnet, too, seemed nervous, and the dark circles under her eyes told him she'd gotten little sleep last night. "I'm not really into fashion or Hollywood gossip magazines, Julian. I didn't bring a book because I don't think I can concentrate."

"Then stop and buy some light reading from the gift shop. Garnet, you need to take your mind off what may or may not happen in Georgia."

"I don't… Oh, very well." Lifting her chin high, she passed through the security checkpoint and once she'd been cleared, she headed off into the first gift shop in the terminal without bothering to see if Julian was behind her.

He wasn't. He had to strip off his belt with its metal buckle. He still set off the sensors, so he had to unload his pockets of loose change and a money clip before they'd pass him through. Even then he didn't rush to catch up with Garnet. She had every right to be annoyed with him for insisting she buy reading material she didn't want. He wasn't trying to be overbearing, but he was afraid that without something to occupy her mind, she'd spend the entire flight brooding.

They met up in the line to board the plane. He glanced at the sack in her hand. "I see you found a book to your liking."

"Yes," she said sweetly. "A how-to manual written by a psychotic killer."

Julian spun toward her with a shocked expression. Seeing her smirk, he realized that was the rise she hoped to get out of him. Deciding it wasn't too late to play along, he deadpanned "I've read it. The author waits until the end to reveal that he wrote it while in a mental institution."

Garnet laughed—a genuine laugh that broke the tension—and smacked him with her book bag as they handed in their boarding passes. "Ma'am, please show me what you have in the sacks," the attendant instructed her.

Standing behind Garnet, Julian got to see what she really bought. A book of Sudoku puzzles. He thought at the very least he deserved an Academy Award for keeping a straight face.

She'd obviously loosened up since the exchange, which had been Julian's intention. She reached their assigned seats first, and stepped aside. "Julian, you take the window seat. We'll fly out over some gorgeous scenery you won't want to miss."

"Thanks. The day I flew in I was dumbstruck by the number of lakes there were. I couldn't believe it when the captain came on and told us that Alaska has more than three million lakes. I would have sworn Minnesota had the most."

"Remind me never to sit on your trivia team," Garnet teased as they both sat and buckled in. "You know, I really hated having to wait until today to get underway, but I'm glad you had those two days for sightseeing."

"Me, too. And it gave you a chance to tie up loose ends with your job. I still have more than a week left of my leave to help you get settled."

Garnet squeezed his forearm. "I haven't said thank you enough."

"No need." Julian promptly put up his professional barrier. He took the rest of passenger-loading time to fire up his laptop and check his e-mail. When he saw one from Larry Adams that included an attachment, he scrolled straight to it. It was Garnet's case report. He couldn't begin to guess how Larry had managed to copy it, but he scanned the file eagerly. There were portions Larry had underscored in red. Julian flipped back to check dates and to reread those notes. His head shot up and he sucked in a deep breath, and whistled under his breath, forgetting that Garnet sat beside him.

She'd been absorbed watching a man trying to stuff a too-large bag into the overhead bin across the row. "Something wrong?" she asked, turning to Julian. "Is it from your dad? Is it Sophie?"

Julian shook his head. "I shouldn't show you

this," he muttered. "Saturday night, I asked Larry to try to get a peek at your file. He's sent me a copy." Julian angled his laptop so that she could read the screen. "Check the date on the page, then tell me what you think of the part Larry underlined." Julian indicated Gary Savage's notes and a recorded interview with the secretary at Sophie's preschool.

Garnet read the highlighted text. "I thought I told you Barb said she took a call from Dale a day or two after the kidnapping."

"But now skip to one of Savage's later notes where he refers to a phone call from Barb the week before Thanksgiving. She reported receiving a second call from a man she thought was Dale Patton. The caller apparently said he wanted to reassure everyone that his daughter was well."

"Thanksgiving?" Julian heard the shock in Garnet's voice. "Why wouldn't Gary have told me about this?"

"Beats me. According to his note Savage questioned her, and decided she was so rattled she was mistaken. He chalked it up to a holiday crank caller."

"Even so, shouldn't he have given me an opportunity to speak to Barb myself?"

Preferring not to comment on how a fellow

officer chose to handle his case, Julian scrolled down to the next underlined section. "This entry is dated the second week in January of this year." Again he turned the screen toward Garnet.

She gasped. "Barb phoned the station to report a third call from Dale? She left a message with a corporal who said Gary was on vacation." Garnet's jaws snapped shut. "I wish I'd known this when Gary dared to jump on Larry Saturday night. Twice he's made rash assumptions that the calls weren't from Dale. Did he even interview Barb about this call?"

She clasped her hands to keep them still. "Julian, why would Savage keep this from me? After the November contact, why didn't he tap Barb's phone? I know they weren't allowed to continue tapping my line or the school phone beyond the time allotted by the original court order, but..."

Cautioning Garnet to lower her voice, Julian closed the attachment. And at the stewardess's request, he shut off his laptop and tucked it into the seat pocket. "There's no law that says Savage has to share *any* information with you. Early on in a kidnapping case it's fairly easy to get a wiretap. Judges aren't so accommodating a year or more down the road."

"All the same, to me it seems we—he—missed a golden opportunity to trace where Dale was."

"Assuming it was Dale."

"Whether it was him or not, the possibility would have given me hope, don't you see? My holidays were awful. I hated going downtown between Thanksgiving and Christmas. All of the store windows were decked out with toys. Do you know how many TV ads focus on happy families? Christmas Eve, I cried all night."

Sensing she was close to tears now, Julian eased his left arm around her, offering his shoulder as a refuge. He felt a shudder run through her. "I'm sorry I upset you." He stroked her hair, hoping to comfort her.

"I just don't understand why he'd keep phoning Sophie's school. Was he taunting me? I don't know what I ever did to him to deserve this."

"That part does puzzle me." Julian leaned back and tried to look into Garnet's eyes. "There's no mention of the secretary telling police that the caller wanted anything, such as Sophie's immunization record if he intended to put her in school. If his aim was to make you miserable, why not phone you directly?"

"Well, at Sergeant Savage's suggestion, I had my home phone number changed and unlisted to avoid crank callers—and there were a lot at first. I moved, too. Dale wouldn't have known how to reach me, but he could have called my school. That number's the same. I had no reason to go back to Sophie's preschool after I picked up her belongings and cleaned out her desk."

"Tomorrow, before we start surveillance on the family, I'd like you to call Barb. Explain that you've just learned of her two reported contacts with Dale, and see if she can remember any more of what he said."

"I don't know Barb that well."

"She wanted to help you. She tried. Garnet, three contacts by someone on the run is out of character. I'd like to learn as much as we can."

"I suppose you think he had some noble reason. This isn't the first time you've sounded charitable toward Dale. What is it with you, Julian? He stole my child and you're a cop, for heaven's sake."

"I'm only trying to add up the facts. Cases are lost all the time because someone jumped the gun, or didn't close all the loopholes."

"I frankly don't see how that applies. I have sole legal custody of my daughter, and my ex-husband walked out of the preschool with her. Those are the facts."

Julian turned aside and pressed his forehead to the window as the plane taxied down the runway. "We're on our way to see if the little girl in Mosswood is Sophie," he said without enthusiasm.

Garnet's fingers tightened on the arms of her seat when the whine of the engines increased. She didn't relax until after the Boeing 757 was in the air. Staring at the back of Julian's head, Garnet wished she knew what was going on inside his brain. He had a habit of dropping a subject if he chose not to tell her more. Yet he was never discourteous. And most of the time she felt his empathy.

Or was she just falling under his spell? He was fit, good-looking and in a career she admired. A total package she could easily fall for. If she hadn't already learned her lesson with Dale.

The more engrossed Julian became in the land-scape below, the less it appeared he had any intention of restarting their conversation. Settling back against the headrest, Garnet shut her eyes. If nothing else, Julian's comments had her reflecting on the good parts of her marriage, as well as the bad times leading up to its dissolution.

Dale had worked hard on the pipeline. He'd earned good money for a dangerous job. What she earned from teaching back then had gone straight into savings. They'd talked about children early on in their relationship and they'd agreed they both wanted kids. Three or four, they'd decided. Garnet hadn't liked being an only child, and Dale disliked having his only sibling be a generation older. Dale had brought her a dozen roses the day after she told him that she was pregnant.

The early part of her pregnancy was rough. Dale helped a lot around the house. He painted and furnished the nursery while she sewed curtains and made a quilt for the crib. But he changed after he and a number of other men were laid off when the pipeline connected the final section to the oil fields.

He was spending more time out of the house, but was it because of his growing unhappiness in their marriage, or was she to blame? As the financial pressures mounted, she'd begun harping at Dale. Talking about it at lunch with her teacher friends fed her anxiety. And Dale added to it, joining that biker crowd. She'd refused to meet them on general principles.

Dale wanted her to get to know some of the

wives, to see that there were good people in the club. She could have made time. But she never did.

Unable to stand reliving the past, Garnet opened her Sudoku book. It helped to concentrate on numbers rather than painful memories. Julian had been right to say she needed something to take her mind off looking for Sophie.

THEY TOUCHED DOWN in Minneapolis on schedule and without incident. "I'll be glad to stretch my legs," Julian said. The rows of passengers in front of them had begun to disembark. The line was slow to reach them.

"How long do we have till our next flight?"

"Two and a half hours. Shall we find our gate and then go grab something to eat?"

"I'm not hungry, but I could go for a cup of coffee."

Julian followed her up the passenger ramp. "Caffeine on an empty stomach isn't the best prescription for a cross-country flight, Garnet."

She made a face at him. "I eat when I'm hungry."

"In other words, stop bugging you?"

Garnet laughed. "It's okay. It's sweet of you to care. I'm not used to anyone worrying about me."

Julian thought that was sad, but he kept it to himself.

When they checked the departure board at the gate, they saw a notice that their flight had been delayed.

"I wonder why. Wait here a minute and I'll go ask." Julian was shuffled between three clerks and finally returned with news. "Apparently there's been tornados moving through Iowa, Indiana and Ohio. As of now, there's an expected delay of up to one hour. That could still change, however. We need to keep our ears tuned to announcements. I'll phone my folks with the closest estimate before they need to leave home."

"Is it a long drive for them?"

"Long enough. Plus Atlanta is one of the busiest airports outside of New York and L.A., so I need to give them as much advance notice as possible."

She glanced at her watch. "Since we have time on our hands, maybe I'll try to get hold of Barbara Davison now, instead of waiting until tomorrow. You've convinced me."

"You have the number? I mean…do you think she's still at school?"

"The preschool is a year-round one. But they take

a two-week break when public schools let out so families can go on vacation if they have children in other grades. There's a possibility, of course, that Barb's family is doing the same thing. I have their son in one of my classes, and he's Lester Junior, so I can get the number from directory assistance if it's listed."

"Sounds like a plan. Here, want to try the Itasca Grille?" Julian asked as they approached a restaurant. "Says American food and a full bar. Or you can choose another place."

"This looks fine." Garnet let Julian give their name. She took out her cell phone and soon had a listing. She waited until they were seated to place the call.

Julian listened with interest to the one-sided conversation when Garnet connected with the preschool secretary.

"Barbara, it's Garnet Patton. Yes, it's been a long time. Listen, I've just heard that you received two calls last winter from a man you suspected was Dale."

Ordering a burger for himself while Garnet talked, Julian asked for coffee for her, and as an afterthought, added a bowl of old-style chicken noodle soup. Let her eat it or not. He knew they weren't going to get anything but pretzels on the flight to Atlanta.

Garnet rooted through her purse while balancing the phone on her shoulder. Guessing she needed to write something down, Julian passed her his notebook and a pen.

"Thanks," she mouthed, shifting the phone to her left ear. She even frowned prettily, Julian thought. He found himself staring at her slender fingers with their pink-polished, close-cropped nails. He was still staring when she hung up and began drumming her fingers on the table. "Well, that was enlightening *and* frustrating. Barbara is positive the caller was Dale. She did wonder why no one from the FBI or local police ever followed up on her reports. When he called in November, he said much the same thing as the first time, two days after Sophie's abduction. Just that Sophie was fine."

Julian leaned forward, stilling her tapping fingers. "The third call was different?"

"Yes. Dale asked if I'd left Anchorage. He said he'd tried our number and was surprised to find it disconnected. Barb thought she'd be cagey and asked for a number where I could reach him. That's when he hung up, and she hasn't heard from him since. The cop she talked to right after asked if she'd tried to hit *69 to pick up the caller's number. Barb wasn't aware she could do that. And once she made her call to the police it was too late."

"Hmm." Julian stroked his chin, which by now had begun growing whiskers. He sat up straight when the waitress arrived with their food.

Garnet reached for her coffee, then glanced up in surprise when the woman placed a steaming bowl of soup in front of her. "But I didn't order soup…." she protested, breaking off when Julian indicated he'd ordered it for her. "Uh, thanks. It does smell delicious," she added, opening a cracker packet.

The waitress asked if they needed anything else as she handed Julian ketchup. "No, thanks. Nothing right now." He smiled. She turned away and he rearranged the bun on his burger. "Mmm, good," he mumbled around the first bite. After devouring half the sandwich, he returned to discussing Dale's phone calls. "Garnet, you asked Ms. Davison if Dale ever sounded like he was gloating. What was her answer?"

Garnet paused, cracker in one hand and soup spoon in the other. "Actually, Barb said no. The first time she said he definitely sounded rushed and she heard noise in the background, like maybe a pneumatic nailer. In December, she said he really seemed concerned with my whereabouts." Crushing a cracker, she snapped, "If he was so frigging concerned, he ought to have just brought Sophie back!"

"Would you have forgiven him?" Julian took another bite of his burger.

"I know you expect me to say that, no matter what, I wouldn't. But we'll never know, will we? Because Dale didn't bring Sophie back."

"No. He didn't. I just wonder if he regrets the way he handled things." Julian shrugged one shoulder as the loudspeaker crackled. He held up a hand. "That's our flight number." He set his burger down, wiped his fingers and listened intently.

Garnet began gathering her purse. "It sounds as if we're being moved to a plane that's leaving earlier."

Across the table, Julian started counting out money. He quickly calculated the tip and picked up his laptop and book. On the way out, he explained their dilemma to the hostess.

"I'll tell your waitress. Do you have time for us to bag your food to carry on?"

"Not really. But thanks for offering." As they dashed to the new gate, Garnet asked between breaths, "Will we be arriving earlier than your parents expect?"

"Perhaps. Before we board I'll confirm our landing time. If it's a matter of half an hour I won't bother phoning them." Which did turn out to be the case. They would arrive at Hartsfield an estimated thirty-five minutes before their original flight.

"I haven't flown since the day Jenny and I moved to Anchorage. Is this the usual way airlines do business now?"

"They've always had to fly between storms. Now they have fewer flights, fuller planes, more overbooking and the occasional bomb scare. You need to go with the flow or it'll raise your blood pressure."

Settled on board for the final leg of their journey, Garnet touched Julian's hand, sending a thrill up his arm.

"Pinch me so I'll know this isn't a dream," she said. "You should feel how fast my heart is beating just from imagining that by tomorrow I may get to see Sophie. See her, hold her, hug her. Oh, Julian, you have no idea what that means to me."

He felt her pulse flutter in her wrist. Because

cops knew things rarely went according to plan, he said nothing, but held her hand next to his heart for as much of the flight as was humanly possible.

HIS PARENTS WERE EARLY. They were the first people Julian saw as he and Garnet left the baggage area. "Mom. Pop." Julian embraced first one then the other. Garnet hung back, so he reached back and dragged her forward. "This is Garnet Patton. Garnet, this is my mother, Beth, and my pop, Samuel. Call him Sam."

"I'm pleased to meet you," she said softly. "Thank you so much for letting me barge in on you for a few days."

"My word," Sam Cavenaugh exclaimed, squeezing his wife's shoulder. "The minute I saw you, Garnet, I became even more convinced that the child I saw is your daughter. Same face shape, smile and everything." The iron-haired man nodded his head up and down, grinning all the while.

"Truly?" Garnet was so overcome with joy she could barely breathe.

"Pop, you know they say everyone in the world has a twin. I wish you wouldn't go building Garnet's hopes." Julian sounded fiercely protective, and he acted it, too. He anchored a supportive arm around Garnet's waist.

His mother arched one eyebrow in response. Beth Cavenaugh shooed the men off to load the bags into the car. She welcomed Garnet with a big hug. "We want you to make our home your home while you're here."

"That's so nice of you," Garnet murmured. She brushed a damp trail of tears from her cheek as she and Beth followed behind the men.

"Are you both starved?" Beth asked once they were on their way. "I have cold cuts at home if you are."

"I'm always hungry." Julian playfully jerked a thumb at Garnet, adding, "Not this twig. While she's with us, your mission, Mom, is to fatten her up."

They all laughed, and that set the tone for easy banter for the rest of the drive to Mosswood.

Once there, Beth again left the men to wrestle the bags as she offered to show Garnet around.

"Your home is lovely," Garnet exclaimed at the end of the tour.

"It's too much house for us at this stage. Julian is the only one of our four children who has expressed interest in buying it. But his job is in the city, a next-to-impossible commute."

"Why would he want such a big house?" The question popped out before Garnet could consider the implications.

Beth smiled. "My fervent prayer is that he'll find a nice woman who'll want to settle down here and give us lots of grandbabies." She sighed. "A vain hope, I'm beginning to think, unless you know something I don't."

"Oh, no. We mostly talk about my case." Yet as the words fell, Garnet realized that they weren't entirely true. She and Julian had experienced a connection she wouldn't attribute to just her case.

"Well, dear, this will be your room while you're here," Beth said, shoving open the door to reveal cheery, flower-sprigged wallpaper and curtains and bedspread to match.

"I'm more exhausted than I expected to be. Perhaps because of the time difference and the anxiety of flying—plus the possibility of seeing my daughter tomorrow. Have you seen Sophie?" Garnet asked eagerly.

"No, but I'm crossing my fingers that it all turns out for the best."

"You're all so kind. I know it's early but I think I need to turn in. Please thank Julian again for allowing me to come here. Tell him I'll see him in the morning." One of the men had already set Garnet's suitcases in the room, so she stepped inside and closed the door.

Downstairs, the men built sandwiches and made plans for Julian to take Garnet to the Hackett home around 10:00 a.m., when Sam expected to deliver their mail. "I'll make some excuse to take the mail to their door. The girl always runs to the window. Son, you make sure Garnet is close enough to ID the kid, okay?"

"I'll try. I hope she can sleep tonight. And that I can, as well. I'm still not sure we're doing the right thing, Pop. What do you think?"

"I think we're about to reunite two deserving people." Smiling, Sam bit into his Dagwood-style sandwich.

CHAPTER SEVEN

JULIAN AND HIS MOM were in the kitchen talking and drinking coffee when Garnet came downstairs carrying the teddy bear. "There you are. I can't believe I slept this late. I'm so sorry, Mrs. Cavenaugh, I didn't mean to be rude."

"Call me Beth. I'm happy you were able to sleep in a strange bed. Julian was just saying he had worried you wouldn't get any rest at all."

"The bed was heavenly. Oh, thanks," she said, taking the mug of coffee Julian handed her. "And the room was so quiet! I didn't hear a thing from the moment my head hit the pillow to when the light from the window woke me up. At home I hear every little noise from the units near mine."

"I was working in real estate when we built the house, so we had access to a wonderful architect. Sound insulation was one of the things we insisted on. It's absolutely crucial with a big family. Not to change the subject, Garnet, but a minute ago I talked Julian into having Belgian waffles with me. Is that okay with you? If you'd prefer bacon, eggs and toast, I'll fix that while the waffles cook."

"Goodness, don't go to any trouble on my account. Coffee will do me." Garnet set the stuffed toy on the center island and checked her watch. "It's nine-fifteen. You said we'd meet your father at ten, Julian. Shouldn't we be leaving?"

"There's time to eat. The house isn't far from here. Mom said she has fresh strawberries and cream for the waffles, or an apple-apricot sauce. Which would you like?"

The table had already been set for three, Garnet saw. She sank down on the chair Julian pulled out for her, but had difficulty concentrating on anything other than the effect his aftershave was having on her. "Strawberry," she finally managed to say.

"It's unanimous." Beth took a bowl of sliced strawberries out of the fridge and set it in the middle of the table. A fresh berry aroma competed with Julian's aftershave and eventually won Garnet's attention.

"It seems early for vine-ripened berries," she said. "But then, I've gotten used to the growing season coming later in Alaska."

Beth moved easily around the country kitchen as Julian talked about his visit to the forty-ninth state. "Last night I showed Pop pictures of the salmon I caught. Josh and Tag will die of envy." His laugh was pure glee. "I swear, Mom, I didn't even scratch the surface of what there is to do and see in Anchorage, let alone the rest of the state. When it comes to outdoor recreation, Alaska beats Georgia, hands down. I wish I'd had time to hike to one of the lakes."

"Maybe you'll go back again sometime to visit Garnet." Beth glanced over her shoulder before she transfered a hot waffle from the sizzling griddle to a plate.

Julian let his gaze travel leisurely over the woman seated on his right. He couldn't tell if it was because of his mother's casual suggestion or the rose-colored mock turtleneck she wore, but there was a decidedly pink tint to Garnet's cheeks. "Um…maybe I'll convince her to give Georgia a try," Julian said softly. "Nice as Alaska is, Georgia's home."

The pink in her cheeks deepened. Garnet swatted Julian's knee. She was afraid his mother would draw the wrong conclusion about their relationship and hissed as much in his ear.

His only response was to broaden his grin.

Beth delivered the first waffle to their guest. "Julian, the whipped cream is in the white bowl in the fridge. Hand it and the butter to Garnet while I cook your waffle."

He complied, telling Garnet not to wait when it appeared she wasn't going to butter her waffle until he and his mom had theirs.

"Yes, eat while yours is hot," Beth said. "If there's a downside to waffles, it's that I can only make one at a time."

"These are big. Half of one is plenty for me. Julian, pass me your plate and we'll share."

"Only because I know you eat like a mouse. But I can be stubborn, too. When mom dishes up mine, you're taking half of it and no fussing."

Beth eyed them speculatively. "You two put me in mind of Taggert and Raine, the way you squabble. Except they've been at it since third grade."

Julian paused while Garnet put half her waffle on his plate. "Tag's my younger brother, and Raine's his wife," he explained for her benefit. But his mother's comment made him think. Tag and Raine had been in love forever. "Well, I certainly have enjoyed spending time with you—after the first meeting, I mean. I swear you would have killed me that day, if you could," Julian remarked, nudging Garnet.

"Praise the Lord," Beth exclaimed in her engaging Southern accent. "Julian is a master at escaping from the women any of us bring home. And believe me, Garnet, his brothers, sister and I have brought plenty."

"Mom, for cripes sake!"

Garnet smiled and gestured with her fork. "What I love—what's let me relax is—the way you tease each other. In my home, meals were eaten in total silence. My father sat at the head of the table, his nose in an astronomy book. My mother wrote chemistry formulas on a yellow legal pad. I could have whatever I scrounged from a cupboard so long as I did it quietly."

That statement made Julian ache on her behalf. Beth delivered his waffle, and opened her mouth to say something to Garnet, but the phone rang, causing her to break off and backtrack to answer it.

"Julian, it's your dad. He wants to talk to you. Come quickly, he sounds upset."

Scooting his chair back, Julian set down his knife.

Tensing, Garnet followed his progress to the phone even as she finished buttering his hot waffle for him. His side of the conversation sent chills up her spine and caused her hand to shake as she reached for the bowl of berries.

"What do you mean the house is empty, Pop? I thought you said the boys were riding their bicycles in the street yesterday."

Beth had her waffle on a plate, but she stopped in the act of unplugging the griddle. Her eyes slid from Julian to their guest. Aware the call didn't bode well for Garnet, Beth crossed the room and placed a bracing arm around the younger woman's trembling shoulders.

"Damn, that makes me sick, Pop. What tipped him off? I wonder. No, you can't blame yourself. You couldn't have known. Did they leave a forwarding address at the post office? Well, that's not surprising." Julian cast a worried glance toward Garnet. "Yeah, thanks for the heads-up. There is stuff I can check. If, as you say, the curtains are open and the house is empty, Hackett must've had a truck. There aren't too many truck rental sites in Mosswood. I'll look into that. Do me a favor, ask neighbors if they saw him loading up."

Hanging up, Julian's eyes remained locked on Garnet. "You heard," he said.

"How…could this happen?" Reaching for Sophie's bear, Garnet hugged it tightly.

Julian crossed the room and wrapped his arms around her, whispering fiercely in her ear, "If I ever doubted that Lee Hackett was Dale Patton, or that his girl was Sophie, that's all changed now."

"She was so close, and now she's gone," Garnet cried. "I've traveled all this way for nothing."

"Don't count us out yet," Julian said, releasing her slowly. Gazing down at her white face, he brushed back her flyaway hair. "Give me time to regroup and make some calls. I'm hoping Pop will learn something useful from neighbors."

"It's like Dale knew I was in town. How could he, Julian?"

"Damned if I know. But wait, maybe…my first day in Anchorage, I stumbled across a biker group at lunch. I asked about Dale and got the distinct impression people in the room knew more than they let on. They were a closemouthed lot. It's possible your ex had one of them keeping an eye on you."

"For over a year? Without me knowing?"

"People hiding out build networks, Garnet. We see it a lot in law enforcement. Keep in mind that the hunted eventually wear down, or screw up and make a mistake. Listen, you and Mom finish breakfast. I'll do some digging, then meet Pop, and we'll put our heads together. Maybe we'll come up with something that will help us find Dale again."

"I couldn't eat," Garnet said, staring at her cooling waffle. "I want to go with you, Julian. At least see where Sophie's been living."

"What's the point? Mom, help me convince her I can do this better on my own." He gently pressed Garnet back into her seat. Brushing a kiss over her hair, Julian strode from the room.

Garnet jumped when the front door slammed.

Almost at once, both women heard Julian's Ducati rumble and then roar out of the driveway.

"He's right," Beth said after the noise faded. "Although, I'm sure if I was in your shoes, I wouldn't be able to eat, either. I'll dump these waffles in the compactor and fix us energy drinks. I often have them if I'm going out to show a property early in the morning."

"That's very kind of you. I'm...*numb* would describe the way I'm feeling." Garnet looked up, revealing dark, glistening eyes.

"Once I whip up the drinks, we need to get out of the house. There's a small chapel maintained by our church. It's a great place to restore the spirit. In raising four children to adulthood, I've worn grooves in the kneelers. I'll leave Julian a note in case he comes back before we return."

"I prayed all the way here. For all the good it did," Garnet said, her voice cracking.

"Oh, honey, prayer is never wasted. You have Julian in your corner, and I'm not just being a proud mother when I say he's an excellent detective."

Garnet couldn't seem to sit still and she began pacing around the kitchen. "I wish he'd been on my case from day one. I put so much faith in Sergeant Savage, the officer in Anchorage. He seemed dedicated and helpful in the beginning. But now it looks like he dropped the ball somewhere along the line."

Beth had been cleaning up as Garnet paced. She dumped milk and powder from a can into a blender with the berries they hadn't used. She pressed a button and in seconds poured a frothy mixture into a pair of travel mugs. Closing Garnet's chilly right hand around one mug, Beth said, "I'll find my car keys and write Julian a note, then we can go. How about we swing past my salon after visiting the chapel and see if anyone has time to give us each a body massage. Bring the bear if you like. I assume he belonged to your daughter."

"Yes. I was hoping she'd remember Bear-bear, even if she's forgotten me."

"If ever I have an opportunity to get my hands on the man who made your life so miserable, I'll haul him to the courthouse by his ears," Beth said angrily.

"If you were me, Beth, could you ever forgive him? Julian mentioned the trauma caused to children when parents fight over custody. I know Sophie loved us both. But I'm not sure I could stand it if she's been *happier* living with Dale these past fifteen months. And worse, what if she ends up hating me if he's sent to prison?"

"I'll let you in on a secret about Julian. He's in a difficult line of work for an eternal optimist. Our three youngest accept that this isn't a perfect world. Julian is constantly disappointed by man's inhumanity to his fellow man, woman and child. He thinks the world can be made better through negotiation."

"I wish I were a big enough person to say I'll negotiate with Dale if we find him. I'm not sure that I am."

"That sounds like a dilemma to place in God's hands, dear."

They went into the garage and Beth backed her car

out onto the street. In no time, she pulled into the parking lot of a well-tended church. "If you've finished your energy drink, leave the mug in the cup holder."

To her surprise, Garnet had drained her mug. Fitting it in the holder, she straightened Bear-bear's plaid bow and one floppy ear. "I think coming here was good for me, Beth," she said, propping him on the console before exiting the car. "I feel calmer already." She sighed as she shut her door. "Rather than my mother or Dale's mom, neither of whom are interested in my state of mind, or what's going on with him…I wish you were Sophie's grandmother."

"Well, God does work in mysterious ways." Beth hooked arms with Garnet, patted her hand, and led her down a gravel path to a quaint chapel.

ACROSS TOWN, Julian peered in the windows of the house the Hackett family had vacated. The small clapboard home sat back from the street, and mostly out of sight from the houses on either side, courtesy of thorny hedges.

There was one odd thing Julian noted—the interior looked spotless. Nothing like homes he'd seen before that had been abandoned in a hurry.

Because he had a passing acquaintance with the couples on either side of the rental, Julian decided to make some inquiries.

"If we hadn't seen the boys walking to and from school," Don Bergstrom said, "Ella and I wouldn't have known Ralph Minton had rented out the cottage."

"Minton owns that house?" Julian turned to study a two-story Victorian home across the street, hidden in a thicket of old growth trees. "I wonder if Ralph knows where they went. I thought first of you or Duffy."

"Forget Duffy. He's lost his hearing and lives in a fog."

"Thanks, Don. I'll go talk to Ralph."

"Did Hackett owe you money?"

"No, nothing like that. I have a friend visiting who thinks he might know him from Alaska. Thought I'd check. If it is the right guy and he's still in the Atlanta area, I'll get them together." That seemed to satisfy Don, so Julian jogged over to the Minton house.

"Well, hello, Julian," Ralph said after answering the younger man's knock. "Neighbors said you'd taken Sam's route last week. Is his knee bothering him again?"

"He's just fine." Julian tucked his hands in his

front pockets and spun the same tale he'd given Don Bergstrom.

"Sorry, I don't know where they went. Wasn't exactly a sudden move. Lee rented the cottage on a six-month lease. He didn't give a lot of references, but he paid cash up front. I looked the place over this morning after I found the key tucked inside my morning paper. They left the house in better shape than they found it. I can't complain, except this means I need to find another tenant."

"Did you question why he had no references?"

"Can't say I did. A lot of folks losing jobs these days. I assumed the poor guy was living off his savings. I was glad I could give him a break. That's a big asset of country living, Julian."

"When I rented my condo in Atlanta, I had to fill out all kinds of information. You know, list next of kin and phone numbers and all that."

"Hackett did list next of kin. His mother-in-law, I think. Let me get the form."

Julian waited on the porch, hoping this would be the lead he was looking for. Minton returned with a partially filled-out lease form. "They listed a Mrs. Leland Carter in Macks Creek, Missouri, as next of kin. Liza Hackett's mother, it says."

The name was familiar to Julian. Then he remembered he'd delivered a package from someone by that name to Toby Roberts. "She list a phone number?"

"By golly, no. A post office box is all. And if I recall from my traveling salesman days, Macks Creek is a blip on a back road out of Springfield."

Thanking Ralph, Julian left and drove along the mail route until he located his dad.

"Where have you been?" Sam asked, tucking mail back into his hand cart. "I phoned home twice in the last hour."

"I went to look at the Hackett house and to talk to the neighbors. I left Mom and Garnet at home. Where do you suppose they got off to?"

"If that little gal was as upset as I expect she was, Beth probably took her shopping. That's how your mom copes."

"Garnet *was* upset. So much so that shopping's the last thing I'd think she'd feel like doing. She's down-to-earth, Pop. Finding Sophie is pretty much all that's on her mind."

"I understand. Say, seems you got to know her pretty well, Julian. Just watch how involved you get in her life."

"Why? Didn't you like her? You haven't given her a chance. You can't judge her based on last night! She's hanging on by a thread."

"Don't get huffy. I'm not criticizing her. She seems nice enough. I'd warn you off any woman in her situation. Even if you get lucky and find her daughter, the fight that'll follow is sure to bankrupt her emotionally and financially."

"It doesn't have to happen that way. She and her ex are both adults, and both obviously love Sophie a lot. A good mediator could facilitate shared custody, Pop."

"You? Son, don't try it. There's too much water under the bridge, so to speak."

Julian stubbornly clenched his jaw.

Sam gripped his eldest son's shoulder. "Well, things being what they are I hope you've had better luck than I have. I talked to Beau Duffy when I delivered his mail. He's right next door but claims he didn't see or hear anything. I wouldn't want to live near Beau and need help. Here's a question. Since you have to go back to Atlanta next week to work, what's the next step? Will Garnet stay on? She's welcome, of course. If you need my help or your mother's, you know you've got it."

"I have one lead and it's slim. Ralph Minton had the name and a P.O. box listing in Macks Creek, Missouri, for Mrs. Hackett's mother, Mrs. Leland Carter. I made a few calls while I was hunting you up. Mrs. Carter is a widow, and apparently lives on her late husband's disability. No phone number. You won't like this, Pop. I also contacted my boss. The chief extended my paid leave for two weeks. If I can't prove anything in that time, I'll give up the chase and Garnet will have to go home. Meanwhile, I'm going to Macks Creek."

"You're going to Missouri? You flying into Springfield?"

"Nope. Ralph Minton knows the area well. He said it's as easy to drive. I figure two days up and two back on my bike. That'll give me a chance to work out if we should take further action ourselves. Or if we ought to contact a communications specialist with NCMEC. Or notify the FBI," he added with more reluctance.

"You'll have to forget any negotiating if you do that, Julian."

"I know, but maybe I can sweet-talk information out of Mrs. Carter. That'll be the deciding factor. My first concern has to be what's best for the kid. In this case, though, I also want what's best for Garnet."

"So, it's like that is it?"

Julian nodded as he threw a leg over his bike. "The hell of it is, Pop, I can't say when, or how, or why, but she's different than other women I've met. Her well-being is really important to me."

Sam grasped the handle of his mail cart. "Love sneaks up like that."

"Love? Who said anything about love?" Julian looked so startled, Sam laughed.

"You did. Maybe while you're on this trip, you'll dig deep enough to see how hard you've fallen. Take care on the road, son. It's a long drive. Sure you wouldn't rather fly to Springfield and rent a car?"

"I need to feel the wind in my face. I guess I have more cobwebs to clear out my head than I thought."

THE HOUSE WAS EMPTY when Julian arrived home. He found his mom's note in the kitchen and was glad she'd taken Garnet under her wing. Although he was more than a little disappointed that he'd have to leave her a message telling her about his plans. As he climbed the stairs to pack, Julian realized that it was more than that. He would miss not seeing Garnet before he left. She'd want to go, but he'd rather go alone.

His cell phone buzzed. He quickly reached for it, thinking it would be Garnet or his mom calling to let him know when they were coming home.

It was Larry Adams. "Hey, Larry, what's up? Yeah, we had an okay flight. No, we haven't found him yet." Julian quickly filled Larry in on their run of bad luck. "Really? And what did Savage say when he cornered you? Interesting. You're right, it's odd. I don't know what to think. Now that he's met Garnet, Pop is more convinced than ever that the girl we saw is Sophie. The family was here yesterday, and gone today. I'm about to leave to check on a lead in Missouri. Thanks for covering for Garnet. Call me again if you find out any more from Savage." Julian closed his phone and chewed his bottom lip as he tried to process what Larry had just told him.

Unsure what to make of it all, he decided to forge ahead with his plan. He had gathered enough clothes for four days, and was pulling his leather jacket from the closet when he heard the garage door open.

Garnet's voice drifted up the stairwell to his bedroom. Julian recognized the happy flutter of excitement in his stomach. He wouldn't have to leave without collecting a last memory of Garnet's sweet smile, and with a little luck, a goodbye hug, after all.

Julian caught a glimpse of himself in the mirror over his dresser, and was blindsided by his sappy expression. Oh, yeah, his pop had him nailed. He'd fallen hard, but it wasn't as uncomfortable as he'd thought it would be.

Making his way down the stairs, he called, "I'm home. I read your note."

Two heads appeared around the kitchen door frame. "We didn't expect you back so soon," his mother said.

Garnet stepped into the hall. "Are you going somewhere?" she asked, eyeing his jacket and saddlebags.

"To Missouri." He condensed his morning discoveries into a couple of sentences. "I honestly have no idea what I'll find there, if anything. But it's the best lead we have," he added somewhat hesitantly. "Unless you count the far-fetched story I just heard from Larry. Apparently, Sergeant Savage tried to grill him about your whereabouts. Savage claimed he needed to find you because he'd come across evidence suggesting Dale left the country."

"What?"

"Yeah, the Cayman Islands, he said."

Garnet's eyes widened, but she shook her head. "How is that possible? Your father said he saw the children at the house yesterday."

"It does seem like a long shot. It's up to you whether or not to touch base with Savage. It's possible he made up that story to try and implicate Larry—to sucker him into admitting we'd meddled in your case. Of course, Larry played dumb. I knew I shouldn't have involved him. He's promised to keep his ears open. He'll phone me if he finds Savage was telling the truth. In the meantime, I'll go see if this woman in Missouri can tell us anything useful."

"Wait. I want to go with you, Julian." Garnet slipped past Beth and emerged a moment later carrying the stuffed bear. "Let me run upstairs and see if I packed a jacket. It's a lot cooler today than you said it would be this time of year."

Beth gestured toward the hall closet. "I have a dozen jackets, Garnet. Feel free to take your pick." She opened the closet door and pulled out a poplin car coat and a buttery, short-waisted leather jacket.

Julian frowned. "I think she should stay here, Mom. It's a long trip and I'm traveling by motorcycle."

"Oh." Garnet stopped with one hand gripping the newel post. "I *have* ridden before. Do you have a second helmet? And if not, there's probably a store in town that sells them."

Julian turned to his mother for help. She shrugged. "If I were Garnet, I'd go. And Julian, maybe the mother-in-law will be more inclined to talk to another woman than to you."

"Hmm. I hadn't thought of that." What Julian *was* thinking about was having Garnet glued to his back for four days. He wasn't sure his libido could handle that, especially after what he'd finally admitted to himself. And the drive required at least two nights on the road.

As if reading his mind, Garnet paused on the upper landing. "How long would it take to reach Missouri? You haven't packed enough for an extended trip."

"If I don't leave ASAP," Julian grumbled, "I'll be stuck trying to locate Mrs. Carter's house after dark tomorrow."

His mother nudged him toward the kitchen. "Come help me fix sandwiches for you to take along while Garnet gets her things together. I know you'll travel the country roads. You'll save time taking food you can eat at a roadside picnic table."

"Okay, okay. I know when I'm being double-teamed. Sandwiches it is. But I'm a little worried about the weather. I hear the wind picking up."

Beth turned on the small TV in the kitchen. "I'll start the sandwiches and you check the Weather Channel. You could take my car, you know."

"Near as I can tell," he said a few minutes later, "we may cross the tail end of a rain squall passing through Tennessee. The main storm should be well over the Carolinas by the time I hit Chattanooga. I plan to keep on Highway 41 to Nashville, and stop there tonight. With an early start in the morning, I figure we'll make Macks Creek by midafternoon. I hope for Garnet's sake this doesn't turn out to be a wild-goose chase."

"You don't think the Hacketts flew to Grand Cayman?"

"I strongly doubt he'd lay out the extra dough to go there when he could accomplish the same thing more cheaply by going to Aruba or the Bahamas. Neither of those has extradition agreements with the U.S."

"True," Beth acknowledged as she tucked the sandwiches and a few bananas into a canvas knapsack and handed it to her son. "Why would this Sergeant Savage lie to your friend?"

Julian shut off the TV. "That's the sixty-four-thousand-dollar question. Times like now I wish I had a crystal ball."

Garnet entered the room in time to hear his last statement. "If I had a dollar for every time I wished that since Dale left with Sophie, I'd be a millionaire. Is there a way to check flight manifests on planes flying to Grand Cayman today?"

Having gathered all of the gear, Julian stopped halfway to the door. "Yes. If you pick up the phone and call in the FBI." He paused, giving her time to process that. "Garnet, honest to God, I could be wasting your time going to Missouri. I started out just wanting to protect Pop. Now all I want is for you to get Sophie back. Maybe I'm not the best person to help you."

She seemed to waver. Beth glanced from one to the other. "Garnet, you hadn't come downstairs when I asked Julian if he thought they'd gone to the Caymans. He pointed out that your ex could have achieved the same results for less money by flying to Aruba or the Bahamas."

"I see. But I can't figure out why Gary would make it up. On the other hand, he hasn't produced any leads in a while. He also didn't tell me Barb Davison reported those additional calls from Dale. Maybe he's worried about his skin, if you and Larry prove he botched the case. I've made up my mind," she said. "Let's visit this woman in Missouri. If it's a dead end, I'll have to consider contacting the local FBI office. I'm sorry, Julian. I owe your dad, but I can't afford to let our one lead go cold."

"That's more than fair," Beth rushed to say. "Sam's only concern from the beginning was your daughter, and not any consequences to himself. I choose to think the candles we lit at the chapel today are guiding you to Missouri. Good luck. Be safe." She ushered them out the door, then watched Julian attach the saddlebags to the bike. Beth lifted her hand after they'd donned helmets, and Garnet had swung onto the Ducati behind Julian.

Julian returned his mother's wave. His mind should've been on what lay ahead, or even on trying to figure out where Lee Hackett had gone. But all Julian could think about once Garnet's arms circled his waist and he felt the heat of her body against him, was wanting to be her rock. She hadn't had a lot of dependable people in her life, and Julian intended to be a man she could lean on. He'd been alone for a long time, and suddenly he didn't want to be any longer.

CHAPTER EIGHT

TALKING TO JULIAN on the bike proved to be impossible. Garnet had forgotten how the wind would blow her words right back. She'd thought it might be painful to travel on a motorcycle, because of the way she associated them with Dale, and with him taking Sophie away. But tucked behind Julian, with his body sheltering her from the wind, Garnet felt her concerns fade away. She quickly remembered how to lean with Julian when he followed the gentle curves of the country road. She felt connected—felt a part of him. And it was a marvelously liberating feeling. At last she was taking an active role in looking for Sophie.

Julian skirted Atlanta, but it was still interesting to Garnet to see the tall buildings in the distance. She imagined him working the city streets, helping to keep residents safe. Until now, she hadn't been aware how protected Julian made her feel. Since

Dale had absconded with Sophie, her life had been in constant turmoil. She'd kept teaching out of necessity, but in her private hours she ran very close to empty. Emotionally empty. Now, out here on the open road, heading in search of information, she wasn't helpless. Wasn't a victim of circumstance, but a player.

She unconsciously tightened her arms around Julian's waist.

He slowed, moved to the right-hand lane of the highway and glanced back at her.

She couldn't see his eyes through the dark plastic of the helmet visor, but she knew he assumed she'd tried to signal him. Julian's reading of her touch, and his thoughtful response, said something about his character. For a man with a charming but badass look, he had a good core.

Garnet shook her head, freed one hand and motioned him on. He smiled crookedly and mouthed "hang on." He revved up the gas, and Garnet barely had time to grab hold of his jacket again before they took off.

Signs said they were traveling the historic Dixie Highway. They sped past turnoffs to towns with names like Kennesaw, Rocky Face and, listed ahead of them, Tunnel Hill. The road cut through orchards of what Garnet assumed were peach trees.

Time and distance seemed to merge together in a blur before Julian slowed and turned off on a winding trail. Garnet saw why. A rest area. And not a moment too soon. She climbed off the bike, recovered her helmet and pointed to the ladies' restroom.

Julian took off his own helmet as he watched her limp as fast as she could toward the log building at the end of a gravel path. "Ouch," he murmured. Garnet wasn't used to riding the bike for long periods. He worried that by morning she wouldn't be able to keep going. It was a form of being saddle sore, he'd been told. He'd never experienced the problem. He could ride for hours, lost in the whine of the fuel-injection engine.

But that was him being a guy. Garnet would probably be more interested in the sandwiches and bananas his mother had sent along. He pulled off his leather gloves and dug out the knapsack. He chose one of the picnic tables set among the trees away from the road, brushed off the pine needles and debris, and placed the canvas bag on the cleared surface. The rest area was vacant except for them. It was midweek, past lunchtime, and clouds had gotten darker and thicker through the day. "This isn't really picnic weather," he said when Garnet rejoined him.

"Who cares? I'm just glad to be stretching my legs and resting my ears. The farthest I've ridden on a motorcycle before today was a matter of blocks, not miles. Will it screw up your timetable too much if I ask for more frequent breaks?"

Julian passed her a ham-and-cheese sandwich. "I'm sorry I didn't think to stop sooner. You'll have to poke me or something. When I'm riding, I settle into a zone where I can go until I need to stop for gas."

"Must be a guy thing. As a passenger in a car I can talk, read or listen to music. What keeps bike passengers from getting bored?" she asked as she unwrapped the sandwich.

Julian could've told her that having her pressed up against his backside didn't bore him. On the contrary, his mind was occupied with all manner of sensations and ideas. Instead, he said, "I need to wash up, so I'll take my turn in the men's room and be right back. Don't let the squirrels eat my lunch."

Watching him saunter confidently up the path with a masculine roll of his hips made Garnet's mouth go dry. She spotted a water fountain and hurried over to it to wash the bread down.

Possibly it was the isolation of this place that caused her to have inappropriate thoughts about Julian. Inappropriate because although he'd hugged her and delivered a sympathetic kiss or two, he'd never indicated she was anything more to him than a person he'd been roped into helping. And what business did she have to be thinking carnal thoughts about a man whose only interest was in trying to find her daughter?

Jenny and some of Garnet's other friends had tried bringing single guys around to their happy hour gatherings for her. She hadn't been the least bit interested in any of them, so they'd eventually gotten the hint and stopped.

Did women tend to fall for guys in savior roles? Cops, firemen, doctors? Jenny had gone crazy over one of the FBI agents, insisting he was *so* hot, but he'd been too arrogant for Garnet's taste. Julian was a different story. As if to prove it, a thrill ran through her as he emerged from the men's room and started toward her wearing that crooked, welcoming smile she'd come to know so well.

The air had cooled markedly, but even so, she felt her cheeks grow hot at the sight of him.

"You didn't need to wait for me," Julian said, gesturing to her untouched sandwich.

"Childhood lessons are hard to forget," she mumbled, hoping he wouldn't notice her discomfort.

"I hate to rush you, but I don't like the looks of that sky. The TV weatherman in Mosswood said the storm would hold off until tonight, but I'm not convinced he knew what he was talking about."

"Rain, you think?" she asked before biting into her sandwich.

"I'd be happy if that's all we get. I thought I heard thunder in the distance when I came out of the bathroom."

Sitting straighter, Garnet looked up at the sky. It had definitely grown darker. "Well, I guess we won't melt. Rain just won't be pleasant."

"If there's lightning it's more than a matter of being unpleasant riding. It's dangerous. We'll have to find a place to hole up until the storm passes."

"I'm enjoying this break immensely. But you know this country better than I. If you think we should get underway, we can save our bananas for later."

"I'm sorry, Garnet. I know you must be uncomfortable."

"It's okay. I tell myself that every mile gets me closer to Sophie."

"I hope so. Eat up, then. And we can go."

The weather held until after they'd reached Tennessee. Even then Julian had skirted Chattanooga and was well on his way to Hillsboro before it started spitting rain. Hoping to get as far as the outskirts of Nashville before stopping, Julian accelerated a bit.

They'd passed Manchester and were in the hilly area past Beechgrove when the rain fell harder, thunder rolled and lightning cracked. Great bolts of lightning that had Julian looking for the closest place to stay.

In the deluge, he almost missed a small sign advertising vacation cabins four miles away on a side road. They were both drenched by the time he reached the lodge. "I hope they still have cabins to rent," Julian said as he helped Garnet climb off the bike. He nodded toward two cars parked next to the porch, their engines still ticking as they cooled.

Garnet pulled off her wet helmet and together they ran to the shelter of the porch. "I'd pay to stay in their stable as long as it's dry and warm," she said.

A couple exited the lodge carrying a site map and cabin key just as Julian and Garnet reached the door.

"Are you full up?" Julian asked the older woman behind the counter. "I didn't see a vacancy sign, but we're traveling to Missouri on a motorcycle and need to get out of the storm."

"That couple who just checked in came down from Missouri. Sounds like there's flooding in the low-lying areas. And the lightning's scaring the bejeezus out of everyone. I have two cabins left, take your pick." She dangled two keys.

"Uh, we'll take them both," Julian said, extracting his wallet from his wet jeans pocket with some difficulty.

Garnet was cold and wet, and already depressed about not meeting their target destination. Now she felt strangely disappointed about being stuck in a cabin alone. But, of course, Julian would do the gentlemanly thing.

The lodge owner took his credit card and processed two slips. She pulled out a site map and was in the process of explaining where the cabins were when the door opened and a bedraggled family of four trooped in. A man carried a boy of two or three, and the mother cradled a crying baby in her arms. "Our car broke down about a mile south on Highway 41," the man said. "I pushed onto the side of the road, but it won't start. Is there any chance you have a cabin for the night?"

The clerk shook her head. "I'm so sorry. We have nothing left. This couple has just booked the last two cabins."

Partway to the door, Julian turned to Garnet, telegraphing a plea with his eyes.

Trying to hide her elation, Garnet let a second tick past then said, "We're adults, Julian. I see no reason we can't share a cabin for one night."

Julian could've named a dozen reasons off the top of his head. None valid enough to send a family with a baby out in this terrible storm, though. He handed Garnet the map and the key to the farthest cabin. "Why don't you take the saddlebags and go get warm. I'll settle up here and try to find somewhere dry to store the bike."

"We have a shed you could use," the clerk offered. "I'll call my husband downstairs and he can show you where. There'll be no charge."

Garnet had already opened the door when the woman added, "That was a right generous act, Mr. Cavenaugh. You and the lady divorcing or something?"

"Or something," Julian said, hedging as he handed her the other key.

Ah, so he wasn't as distant or as unaffected by her as he liked to let on, Garnet thought, smiling a little after she'd closed the door. Otherwise, sharing space with her for one night wouldn't be such a big deal.

She scurried uphill to the cabin through the still-heavy rain. Inside, she shivered in spite of it being dry. Garnet looked around, doing her best to not focus on the big bed in the center of the room. It was very inviting. Skipping over it, her gaze lit on a stone fireplace on the opposite wall. She found a supply of matches on the mantel, and lit the paper, kindling and wood that someone had thoughtfully prepared. The fire caught and the blaze quickly warmed her.

In general, the big room was spotless. Rag rugs provided welcome splashes of color on the dark hardwood floor. A squat dresser and the headboard of the bed were rough-cut lodgepole pine. A mirror above the single dresser was framed in the same wood. A large, central window overlooked the lodge.

After assessing the small, clean bathroom, she returned to the saddlebags she'd set by the foot of the bed. She was in the process of unpacking her things when the door opened behind her, and the fire flickered wildly.

"You haven't changed yet? You'll catch pneumonia standing around in those wet clothes." Julian turned the night lock before joining her at the saddle-bags.

"It's warming up in here." She gestured to the fireplace with the hand holding her underwear. "Do they serve meals at the lodge? I didn't know whether to plan on putting on clean jeans, or my night T-shirt."

Julian frowned as if he found the question too taxing. Finally, he said, "We'll have to make do with the bananas. Mr. and Mrs. Cheever, the owners, apologized. They're usually only open for fall and winter hunters. In fact, they were in the process of closing up the cabins when the storm drove people off the highway. They felt compelled to give lodging where they could. And they'll provide coffee in the morning."

Bending over to dig in his half of the saddlebag, Julian sniffed and asked, "What smells like peaches? I thought Mom only packed bananas."

"Um, that would be me. Beth treated me to a

lovely massage at her salon this morning. I got to choose from a number of fragrances. This one's called fresh, ripe peaches. You don't like it?" she asked, saving the stuffed bear from falling to the floor, out of where she'd wrapped it in a pair of jeans. "I'm sorry. Your mother's masseuse also gave me samples of shampoo and lotion in the same fragrance to try. They're all I brought."

Julian unsuccessfully tried to block a vision of what happened when he bit into a ripe peach. He squirmed at the decadent thoughts running through his head.

"You smell fine," he half growled, stalking away to hang his jacket in the closet.

"Why don't you shower first?" she said, baffled and hurt by his curt response. "I'll want extra time in there to wash my hair. There's no sense you waiting." Hugging her dry clothes and the bear to her, Garnet crossed to the window and stared moodily out at the pouring rain and the occasional jagged flashes of lightning.

"I want you to take the first turn. And don't sulk. I didn't cause the rain."

"I'm not sulking." She caught her bottom lip between her teeth a moment, then released it with a sigh. "You didn't want me to come along and I probably shouldn't have. Maybe I'm a bad omen for this operation. Or bad luck, or whatever. First, Sophie disappeared the night I arrived in Georgia, then the storm the weather forecaster expected to blow by intensified instead. You paid for two rooms, and I piped up and gave one away. This isn't what you wanted, Julian."

He stopped unbuttoning his wet shirt. Walking up behind her, he clasped her upper arms. His eyes met hers in the reflection in the dark window before he turned her around. "You're taking too much on your shoulders, Garnet. A family can't disappear without a plan already in place. Weather is unpredictable. I didn't *want* two rooms, but I thought it was best for you. Finally, all your talk about peaches gave me ideas…made me want you. Even more than I did before. Made me want to get you in bed, okay?"

She tucked her head against his neck and reveled in the warmth of his skin. "Then why are you acting like such a grouch? I'd rather not be alone tonight, Julian. For miles in the rain, I thought of nothing but having you hold me like this."

He tilted her head up and kissed her. Kissed her so limp the clothing and the stuffed toy she still held fell to the floor between them. When they surfaced,

Julian reached behind her and pulled the drape, blocking out the night and the storm. "I know a way to keep us from arguing over that first shower." Slowly and deliberately he unbuttoned her damp shirt.

She offered no objections when he peeled it and her very wet jeans off her body. She'd already kicked off her boots and was busy working on his shirt. Julian's jeans caught on his boots, and they both almost landed on the floor in their haste to remove them.

He rubbed and kissed the goose bumps from Garnet's skin while they let the shower warm up. "Where's that peach shampoo?" he drawled as the small room filled with steam.

"Wait right here." She dashed out to find the tube among her fallen clothing, and returned with the shampoo, liquid soap and sample lotion, all in the same peachy scent.

Garnet stepped under the spray first.

Julian hung back until she tugged on him and murmured, "I know we haven't discussed health issues. I haven't been with anyone since my marriage ended. And I'm on birth control pills to regulate my cycles."

"And I don't sleep around. I'm clean." The stall creaked as he joined her in the shower and bent to nuzzle her neck. Any inhibitions either of them started out with were quickly rinsed away.

Julian surprised Garnet when he offered to wash her hair. And surprised her further after he was done when he said, "I need you to know I've never felt about any woman the way I feel about you. I want more than just tonight."

She nervously rubbed her palms up and down his wet chest, furrowing the wiry hair flattened by the water. "How can we be sure what we're feeling isn't simply adrenaline?"

"I can only speak for myself. Cops live on adrenaline. What I've come to feel for you doesn't compare. I want to share your life, Garnet. The pain, the joy, everything."

"It wouldn't be fair to you, Julian. I have so little to give, because all of my energy, my emotion has to go to finding Sophie."

He kissed her, turned off the shower and wrapped them both in towels. Holding her close, Julian filtered the fingers of each hand through her hair. "We will find her. I promise."

"I want to believe that. But…please, can we have

tonight for us? Yesterday and tomorrow don't exist. Tonight I want to love you with all I *can* give."

Julian couldn't have refused if his life depended on it. He didn't want to. And he wasn't going to rush the night. He put a log on the fire, then sat with her on the bed and brushed her hair dry, taking time to touch, to kiss, to whisper what would happen later. And their loving was made better by the wait.

JULIAN WOKE UP FIRST, and eased himself up on an elbow to watch Garnet sleep. Reluctantly he slid out from under the comforter and dressed. Bending over her, he kissed her awake. "Good morning, Sleeping Beauty. I'm going down to the lodge to see if I can scare us up some coffee and to get an updated weather report. I figured you'd want some privacy to get ready."

Smiling, Garnet ran her fingers over his lips. Lips that had pleasured her many times and in many ways during the night. "It's thoughtful of you to offer. But don't you think it would be a farce to play the modesty card after last night?" She sat up and flung back the covers. "Give me a minute and I'll go with you. I think you're more of a morning person than I am."

His eyes lit up watching her pull a minuscule scrap of lace up long legs he'd loved having wrapped around him. "One word from you and I'd be an anytime person."

That made her laugh. But she sobered when she found her clean jeans tangled around her daughter's bear at the foot of the bed.

Seeing the many expressions flickering across the face he'd come to love, Julian quit teasing and repacked the saddlebags, except for the bananas they never got around to eating.

The sky was still gray, and water dripped from the roof eaves and from the trees, but they didn't get wet walking to the lodge, where the Cheevers greeted them with coffee. "The Tuttle family left a moment ago. They said to thank you for your sacrifice in letting them have your second room."

"So, the roads are passable?" Julian asked.

"The latest weather report claims the storm has moved on to the Carolinas. If you're heading to Missouri, the freeway should be clear."

Julian finished his coffee. "That's probably a better choice today than traveling rural roads. We won't make up all the time we've lost, but barring delays we could make Macks Creek this afternoon.

Garnet," he said, setting his cup on the counter, "I'll
go bring the bike around." He and Mr. Cheever went
out.

"Are you visiting relatives in Missouri?" their
hostess asked Garnet.

"We're visiting someone to get word on a
relative." Garnet tossed her banana peel in the trash.
"I can't thank you enough for your hospitality. I
don't know what we would've done without you."
Because she heard the rumble of the Ducati, Garnet
made her final goodbyes and hurried out, eager to
see what the woman in Missouri had to say.

Julian had stopped to buckle on the saddlebags.
He saw Garnet wince as she flung a leg over the seat.
Leaning over, he brushed a kiss across her lips.
"Sorry, I know you're uncomfortable. You were
already saddle sore when we stopped for the night,
and we didn't do anything to make it better."

"Um," she murmured, "I'm not so sure about
that. You have better hands than your mother's masseuse."

His smile betrayed his masculine pride. He focused on the joy of the previous night as they
whipped along the freeway. It wasn't until they
crossed into Missouri that Julian's thoughts edged

more into worry. With Macks Creek a couple of hours away, the end of their journey could bring hope, or Garnet might be devastated by another dead end.

A postal clerk told them how to find Mrs. Carter's house. It was a small cottage almost hidden by climbing roses. Julian parked the bike next to a whitewashed fence.

He helped Garnet dismount and remove her helmet. "Are you all right with letting me ask the questions? At least until we see if she has any usable information."

The animation that had livened her face that morning vanished as Garnet merely nodded. She let Julian take the lead and knock on the door. "Mrs. Carter?" Julian asked when a thin, rather plain woman answered the door. "Mrs. Leland Carter?" He introduced himself and Garnet and watched for a reaction to Garnet's name. There was none, so he launched into a story about having stopped in Mosswood to see Lee and Mrs. Carter's daughter, only to discover they'd moved.

"Oh, you know Liza's young man?" The woman stepped out on the porch. "Did you come for the wedding? It was yesterday, I think. I wasn't able to go."

"They weren't already married?"

"No. Well, it's Liza's second marriage. She was married to a pipe fitter before. James Roberts. They lived in Alaska and the boys were born there. Two years ago, James was killed when a logging truck ran into his motorcycle. Liza was devastated. She and the boys came home and moved in with me. She worked part-time in the school cafeteria to keep busy, even though she didn't have to work because of the insurance money."

Julian, who stood arm-to-arm with Garnet, felt the ripple run through her when Mrs. Carter first said her daughter had lived in Alaska. He slid his hand down to grasp hers, to keep her from blurting out something incriminating. "I see," he said to Mrs. Carter. "What took her to Georgia?"

"She met a man—Lee. Isn't that the way women are?" Mrs. Carter glanced at Garnet. "He was an old friend from Alaska, on vacation with his daughter, and Liza went to meet him in town. Next thing I knew they started spending a lot of time together. I only met him after Liza announced he'd found a job in Georgia and they were going off to build a life together. Now she's all walking on clouds because they're getting married."

"Where are they now? Not in Mosswood?"

Mrs. Carter shook her head. "Near there, Liza said. In Wimberly. Hang on. Is something wrong? If you're friends of theirs how is it you didn't know about the wedding and the move?"

Not wanting her to phone her daughter and tip her off, Julian smiled and answered smoothly. "We've just come from Alaska." That part was true. "We knew her husband, er, Lee." That wasn't totally true. He didn't know the man. "We hoped to touch base with Lee before we have to go back to Alaska. This is an earlier contact address we had, so we back-tracked hoping you could help us find Lee."

"Oh, that's nice. Let me get their new address." She disappeared into the house and Julian kept a firm hold on Garnet's hand.

"Here, I wrote it down," Mrs. Carter said when she returned. "Liza said they're buying a house, but that with one thing and another they haven't changed addresses at the post office yet."

Julian pocketed the piece of paper. "We'll try to get back down to Georgia to see them. Would you mind giving us a few days before you mention our visit to your daughter? We'll need time to pick out a housewarming/wedding gift, and we'd like to surprise them." He winked at the woman.

"Oh, certainly. My lips are sealed. I'm happy to hear Liza's new husband has such considerate friends. I thought there might be something strange...well, that's probably a mother being a worrywart. When they were dating I invited Liza to bring him home for supper, but he seemed always to have one excuse or another for not coming. Frankly, I worried that he might be married. I mean, she said he had his daughter with him. I thought it sounded a bit, well, fishy. I mean, why else would he not have wanted to meet me?" She clasped Julian's hand. "Thank you for coming out all this way. It's certainly eased my mind."

Wanting to get back on the road as soon as possible, Julian didn't linger.

As they fastened their helmets, Garnet cast a troubled glance toward the woman now watering geraniums on her porch. "Julian, I hate lying to her. Lee *has* to be Dale, and her instincts were right on. Not that he was married, but that something was wrong with the relationship. Her daughter had to know the situation if she lived in Alaska."

"Maybe not. He could have conned Liza. I just can't figure out what's changed that he'd decide to marry her. Maybe he's getting reckless."

"All the same, I feel sorry for Mrs. Carter. She seems a nice woman. If we don't have to let the authorities know how we found Dale, I'd like to leave her name out of it."

"We will if we can. Come on. We need to leave before she gets suspicious of us hanging around outside her house so long. You have some other decisions to make, Garnet. Namely how we go about confronting Dale. We'll spend one more night on the road, so we can firm up our plans then. For now, let's get going. We can stop for something to eat down the line."

"I hate the thought of having to stop at all. Oh, I know we need to take breaks along the way, but is it possible to drive straight through except for filling the gas tank and such? I'm terrified something will happen and we'll lose him again."

Julian helped Garnet on the bike while he considered her wishes. In her place, he'd be in a hurry to get back to Georgia, too. As it stood, his preference would be to spend another night in her arms. "I understand you're anxious, sweetheart. It's just not a good idea for me to drive thirteen hours in one day—even with breaks. We'll take the freeway to get there faster. Somewhere around the Georgia border we can book into a motel where I can grab a few hours of sleep. Then I'll be good to go straight through to Wimberly. With luck we'll reach their house late afternoon, after Dale gets home from work."

"Of course, that makes sense. I probably won't sleep, but you need rest. Let's finalize everything over supper. I wonder if we can find someplace that serves a good Caesar salad."

They did, and after their food came, Julian asked her straight out if she wanted to surprise Dale herself. "Or should I phone Pop and ask him to call in a family abduction specialist, telling them, though, that we don't want them moving in on Dale until we arrive."

"We've come this far by ourselves. You should probably let your folks know what's happening. I wouldn't be here if not for your father."

They finished their meal and drove through the gathering darkness until another rain squall passed through, forcing them to stop for the night. "I know the weather is frustrating for you, Garnet. But we're not so far from Chattanooga. We'll still make it on time. It wasn't easy but I managed to convince Pop to stay away from the house in Wimberly. It's not his territory at all. So, if Liza or Dale spotted him it could blow everything up in our faces."

"I didn't think I'd be tired, but I am," Garnet said, following Julian into the motel room. "It'll be hard to keep my hands off you," she admitted, "but I don't want to just go through the motions with you, Julian. I'm such a bundle of nerves. Tonight, will you just hold me while we sleep?"

"Of course I will. I'd like to do that every night from here on out."

"I can't make promises, Julian. I can't commit to anything until I have Sophie back where she belongs."

Julian's heart was heavy as he tugged off his boots and jacket, took Garnet in his arms and lay down on the bed with her. He wished like hell he could promise her that everything would go smoothly. Experience had taught him that in domestic cases, unless the two main parties could come to some kind of amicable agreement, people rarely emerged unscathed.

CHAPTER NINE

THEY BURST IN on Patton. He stood alone in a huge, dimly lit room. If there was furniture, it was over-shadowed by the angry man who seemed larger and more menacing than Julian remembered. A violent shouting match erupted between Garnet and her ex, and escalated. Julian attempted to intervene, but he couldn't make anyone listen.

Suddenly a door at the far end of the room opened and a little girl in a nightgown stood there rubbing her eyes. A light shining behind her made her flaxen hair into a halo. Garnet cried out and ran toward the child, who screamed and vaulted into her father's waiting arms. The pain on Garnet's face broke Julian's heart. He wanted to protect her, but when he wrapped his arms around her, she had no substance. He whirled frantically, but Patton and the girl also faded in a hazy mist, leaving Julian helpless and alone....

Unable to breathe, Julian lunged up, clawing at whatever was pinning his arms to his sides. A blanket, he realized, confused by the darkness around him.

"Julian, are you all right?" Garnet's voice calmed the pounding of his heart. He saw her then, standing near a window, outlined by the gray light filtering in. At once, everything flooded back. They hadn't accosted Garnet's ex—yet. They were still at the motel where they'd stopped so he could grab a few hours sleep.

"I think I was fighting dragons," he said, rubbing his face. He had difficulty getting the words out. The dream was still vivid, but it wasn't something he could tell Garnet. "What are you doing up?" he asked, flinging aside the light blanket that had imprisoned him.

Garnet let go of the curtain she'd been holding open, and turned away from the window. "I'm sorry I woke you. I couldn't sleep." She sank down on the foot of the bed.

Even in the weak light, Julian could see that her delicate features were strained. He reached for her and was relieved when she went willingly into his arms. It helped chase away the remnants of the too-real nightmare.

She tucked her head into the curve of his neck and slid her hand over the pocket of the shirt he'd been too tired to remove.

He rested his chin on her soft hair and breathed in the faint, lingering peach scent. Cradling her settled his erratic pulse. "Is it still raining?"

"No. It's stopped. The moon is up. It's either full or almost full. Right before you started thrashing about, I was trying to find the brightest star to make my wish. It's silly, I know. Crossing my fingers, wishing on stars, sending up prayers…I've done all of those things, Julian. But deep down I'm afraid. We are so close to finding Sophie. I'm scared that something will go wrong at the last minute and Dale will be warned off."

"It's natural to imagine the worst, Garnet. But let's try to stay positive. Mrs. Carter said Dale and her daughter have bought a house. That means he's less likely to walk away."

"What if Lee Hackett isn't really Dale? I felt confident we'd find Sophie until Larry phoned. Now that Gary Savage thinks Dale might have left the country, I'm not so sure anymore."

Julian gently caressed Garnet's back. "How then do we explain Mrs. Carter's evidence? She's verified that Liza went to Georgia with a man from Alaska and his daughter. There are too many connecting threads to have it be a coincidence. Anyway, cops don't believe in coincidence."

Garnet sighed heavily. "I suppose. But I can't forget the fact that Gary Savage claims Dale is in Grand Cayman. Until you showed up in Anchorage, there were no new leads in my case."

"All the more reason to suspect this sudden information of his. We know he ignored other leads. Those last two phone calls to the preschool, for example."

"You're right, Julian. I'm worrying too much." She tightened her arms around him and pressed her ear to his heart. "If someone in Anchorage tipped Dale off, it's possible he got spooked, fled, and Mrs. Carter's not aware of it."

"And maybe the moon's made of green cheese."

She smiled tentatively. "You didn't get enough sleep, I can tell."

"I did." He kissed her forehead, the tip of her nose, then found her lips. It wasn't easy but he was careful not to let the kiss turn into anything sexual. He kept it light, but passionate. When Garnet drew back he was already climbing out of bed. "Neither of us is going to rest until this is over. Let me wash up a bit and shave so I look more respectable. Then we'll go straight to the address Mrs. Carter gave us, unless you've changed your mind and want to call in the FBI." His dark eyes met hers.

"I've been going back and forth on that." Garnet bent and switched on the bedside lamp. "I've also thought a lot about what you said in Anchorage. You said kids were the big losers when their parents fight over custody. And yet there was nothing to prevent Dale from pursuing custody legally. Instead, he stole my daughter."

"I can't argue with that, Garnet. There's no excuse for the way he chose to handle the problem. And maybe it's impossible to make this right."

"Maybe. Julian, this could be the last chance I have to thank you for all you've done for me. I know you really wanted your dad to be mistaken."

Her statement hit Julian hard. "That sounds a lot like a goodbye, Garnet." With jerky movements he started his razor. That way he wouldn't have to listen to her spout nonsense.

She was determined to have her say. "If Dale is at the house when we get there, you need to drop me off and go home, Julian. I appreciate you giving me a lift to Wimberly, but if things get nasty, I want you to call the feds, then disappear. For your sake and Sam's." Her eyes filled. "I promise I won't tell the authorities how I happened to track Dale to Georgia. It's the least I can do for you and your dad when you've both done so much for me."

Julian shut off his razor. "As if I'd let you walk into God knows what kind of situation alone. I thought after last night…" Words failing him, he clicked on the razor, turned away and shut the door to the bathroom because he was too hurt to look at her.

Shaken by the depth of his emotion, Garnet waited until the razor shut off and she heard him finish splashing water on his face. Then she opened the door. "Last night meant the world to me. There aren't words to express how much I've come to care for you. But it frightens me, too. Because I'm afraid you could tempt me into giving up my search for Sophie."

Julian dropped the razor and it hit the sink with a crack. In two steps, he held her in his arms. "I would never, never ask that of you, sweetheart. No matter what, we're in this together!"

She cried openly then. Julian had to stay strong,

even though tears stung his eyes. He held her until she was able to collect herself.

Soberly, they gathered their belongings. An understanding passed between them as they got on Julian's bike. They wouldn't speak of this again.

THE RIDE TO Wimberly was uneventful. Julian took sporadic breaks, but neither of them wanted to eat. It wasn't quite 6:00 p.m. when Julian found the address Mrs. Carter had given them and pulled up across the street from the house.

The drapes on the ground-floor windows were open. Three bicycles lay in the front yard—two boys' bikes and one smaller, for a younger child. "That third bike is an interesting development," Julian muttered, kicking down the stand on the Ducati.

As they approached the house, they realized a window was ajar and children's laughter bubbled out. The sound drained the color from Garnet's face.

Smoke from a backyard barbecue curled above the fence and the air smelled of cooking beef. "Suppertime," Julian said, herding Garnet around to a side gate.

"This place looks so normal it's bizarre. Maybe

we've got the wrong house. We can't just barge in on strangers. They'll call the police, and we'll have to tell my story. Then where will we be? Where will your dad be?"

"I *am* the police," Julian reminded. All the same he paused to rub some of the tension from the back of her neck. "Here's how we'll play it, Garnet. If the adults tending the barbecue are the people I saw in Mosswood, I'll flash my badge and put them on the defensive. If it's not them, I'll apologize for our intrusion and be honest about having an incorrect address for friends who just moved to this neighborhood. That may buy us information on any newcomers."

Garnet drew herself up tall and straightened her shoulders. "Fine. Fine. I'm just jittery."

Pressing a hard kiss to her temple, Julian took a deep breath and shoved open the tall, wooden gate.

The yard was large and well tended. The smoky scent of the barbecue was more pungent as they rounded the porch. A man and woman stood next to it, clearly paying more attention to each other than to the sizzling meat. It appeared to Julian as if the two had been kissing, but now parted and glanced around as if sensing they were no longer alone. The minute they sprang apart Julian knew they were the couple he'd seen in Mosswood. He also knew they'd found Dale from the way the man's eyes widened and he swept his new wife behind him protectively.

As he and Garnet approached the couple, Julian pulled out his shield case and flashed his badge. He felt Garnet stiffen, but was proud of her when her first comment sounded civilized.

"You've changed everything about your appearance, Dale. I might have passed you on the street without blinking, but it *is* you. Obviously you know why I'm here. I've come for Sophie."

Dale seemed resigned as he said, "Shedding seventy pounds makes a big difference. The hair, except for the dye job, is more like the old me." Then, whether to buy time or because the meat had begun to burn, he picked up the spatula and flipped each burger. "Liza," he said to the dark-haired woman at his side, "meet my ex-wife, Garnet Patton. I, uh, don't remember your name," he said, glancing at Julian. "Clearly, you're not really a mailman."

"No." Julian shook his head. "My father, Sam Cavenaugh, is the real postman. He delivers cards for the National Center for Missing and Exploited Children, and when he spotted Sophie, he recognized her from one of the cards. For the record, I'm Julian Cavenaugh, Atlanta PD."

Liza's startled gaze slid from Garnet to Julian, then back to her husband. "Dale, I'm so, so sorry. I knew we shouldn't get married, that it wasn't safe. I love you. The legalities aren't important to me."

"They are to me, Liza. And I'm the one who's sorry…for so many things." He set down the spatula, and gently touched her face.

"It's true I went by Lee Hackett in Mosswood," he told Julian. "But here I'm Dale Patton. This probably makes no difference, but I have to get this off my chest before you arrest me. I explained my situation to Liza up front. From day one, she begged me to contact Garnet and ask for shared custody of Sophie. I tried calling our old number, but it had been disconnected and Garnet's new one was unlisted. Truthfully, I didn't know how to proceed. We—Liza, the kids and I—were living a lie, and I hated it. I was afraid to let Sophie go outside. Then I had the idea of trying to find Garnet through Sophie's preschool, so I called a couple of times. When the secretary tried to get my phone number, I panicked at the thought of involving Liza and her boys after all they've been through. Her husband was killed in Alaska, see. The three of us were friends. Dang, I'm rambling." He sucked in a deep breath and took another stab at explaining.

"After my last phone call to the preschool, I knew I had to try a different tactic. A guy I work with recommended a lawyer in Atlanta who'd helped him after his divorce. I made an appointment. The lawyer said I was in a mess. Like I didn't already know. All the same, he met Liza and the kids, and said he'd try to help us. He has an associate out of the country. And he said it was a safe way to test the waters. A way to learn if Garnet was open to discussion, yet not reveal my whereabouts. The associate contacted the Anchorage police on my behalf a couple of weeks ago. That opened a can of worms. The FBI visited my lawyer and tapped his phone. The long and short of it—you're here now, and…I'm just glad it's over."

Garnet frowned at Julian. "So that's why Sergeant Savage acted so suspicious of you at the restaurant. He'd probably talked to that lawyer. And now his story about Dale fleeing to Grand Cayman makes more sense."

"Grand Cayman," Liza exclaimed. "That's where our attorney's associate practices."

Julian spread his hands. "It doesn't matter. Cayman law doesn't apply here. But had Savage been more forthcoming in Anchorage, we might not have traveled to Missouri to see Liza's mother."

"Oh, my poor mom," Liza murmured. "She doesn't have anything to do with all of this."

A lull descended for a moment, until the back door to the house banged open and a trio of kids plus a dog raced down the porch steps. The tallest of the two boys stopped abruptly when he saw the visitors, then grabbed hold of his brother and sister and began pulling them toward the house.

Julian felt a quiver run through Garnet. He steadied her, but she cried out and took two wobbly steps in the kids' direction.

Except for the fact that they weren't in a room, Julian felt he was about to relive the nightmare that had woken him at dawn.

The little girl did break from Gavin's hold. She did hurl herself into her dad's waiting arms. But unlike Julian's dream, Sophie didn't scream. She pointed to Garnet and said repeatedly, "That's picture mommy, that's picture mommy."

"You're right, Leah, girl." Dale smiled at his daughter and tried to clear up the momentary confusion. "We, uh, call Sophie by her middle name for obvious reasons. But Liza and I didn't want her to forget you, Garnet. I had an old wedding photo I used to carry in my wallet. Liza framed it for Leah, and the picture sits by her bed. Every night she includes you in her prayers. God, this is an awful mess," he said, touching Sophie's curly hair.

Garnet reached for her daughter with both arms. Sophie resisted and reared back against her father's chest. Looking terrified, she threw her arms around Dale's neck and buried her face in his shoulder.

Although she didn't make a sound, copious tears began trickling down Garnet's cheeks.

"Garnet," Dale said, his voice unsteady. "You probably won't believe this, but I'm sorry as hell for all the heartache I've cause you. Lord knows I have no right to ask you for any favors. But she wasn't quite four when we left Alaska. Please, give her time to come around. Please!" His voice sounded strained, partly due to Sophie's tight grip on his neck.

Julian thought Garnet might collapse in a heap of emotion. Concerned, he moved in behind her. Not giving a damn what Dale Patton might think of his unprofessional demeanor, Julian embraced the woman he'd come to love.

Liza, who had remained in the background, began jerkily removing overdone hamburgers from the grill. "Everything's on the table for supper, except for the Jell-O salad. I can send one of the boys to fetch it," she said, almost pleading with the other adults. "Perhaps if we all sat down and ate a bite, Leah…er…Sophie might make friends faster."

Julian answered for Garnet, who couldn't seem to quit shaking. "We'll give you a moment to settle your family. Garnet has something out in my saddlebag that belongs to Sophie," he said. "It may help her remember who she used to be. I also need to call my folks so they don't worry. Before we step out front, though, I want your phone number." Julian extracted a pen and his notebook from his shirt pocket, indicating Liza's only choice was to comply.

"This is best, isn't it, Dale?" Liza nudged her husband, who held his daughter so close now that she squealed. His eyes were bright with unshed tears.

Julian felt a wrench in his chest. He shouldn't feel sorry for Patton, who was in a mess of his own making, but Julian tried to imagine being in his position. If this was his child he loved with all his heart, could he swear he wouldn't have broken the law? The very idea made his stomach churn. He was a by-the-rules man, so it should be unthinkable—and yet it wasn't.

"Julian, I don't know what to do." Garnet trailed him out through the gate. "I've been so afraid she'd forget me. And she has. Oh, she has," Garnet said unhappily.

"No, sweetheart, she hasn't. She's a bright girl. Sophie recognized you from the photograph."

Garnet tried unsuccessfully to dry her eyes. "She thinks her name is Leah. She must find my calling her Sophie so confusing."

Julian dug in the saddlebag and handed the stuffed bear to Garnet. "Hold him. I need to phone the folks and bring them up to speed. Can't have Pop thinking something's gone wrong. I don't think you want to have to deal with the feds on top of this."

"No. No. But Julian…I can't eat with them. I'd choke. Sophie's there, but I can't hold her. It hurts so much. I wanted to grab her out of Dale's arms and run as far and as fast as I could. But…that's what he did to me and it's wrong."

Having already punched in the first three digits of his parents' number, Julian jerked his head up and closed the phone. "Garnet, did you hear what you just said? That's likely how Dale felt after the family court judge gave you sole custody and tied his visits to social services. I'm guessing he snapped, marched into her school and took her. It sounded to me as if he regrets his stupidity. Has regretted it for some time now."

"Why didn't he bring her back then, and we could've worked things out?" She picked at the bear's furry padded feet.

"I can't answer that because I'm not him. I've arrested plenty of not-so-bad guys who did dumb things in the heat of a moment. I imagine Dale was terrified that he'd go to prison for the rest of his life. That is a common sentence for kidnapping, Garnet."

She blanched and sank down on the curb. Her back struck the Ducati, almost knocking it off its stand. "We have to go back there and try to work out some kind of compromise. Oh, my brain isn't working, Julian. This is what I feared most. Any fool can see Sophie loves her dad. If I rip him out of her life, she'll blame me—she'll hate me."

"Give me a minute to call home, then we'll discuss this further before we go back." He steadied Garnet with one arm and made his call.

"Hi, Pop. We're in Wimberly. You were right.

Lee Hackett is really Dale Patton, and the girl is Sophie. No, don't phone anyone. Garnet and I are going to try to work something out. If we need help I'll call you back. Otherwise, we'll probably roll in around eight-thirty or nine."

On the other end of the line, Sam Cavenaugh didn't seem sure of what he'd heard. "Not call the authorities? Son, are you certain?"

"For now, yes. We'll need to contact them eventually, of course, when Garnet decides whether to press charges or drop them. The choice is hers. I'm just offering moral support."

They said their goodbyes, and Julian pocketed his phone.

"You're more than moral support," Garnet informed him. "You're my rock. I need you to tell me what I should do."

"I wish I could, but like I told Pop, it's a decision only you can make, sweetheart. I also have selfish reasons for stepping aside. I want to be a part in your life, but if I told you what to do and later you decide it's wrong, I don't want you to blame me. But I'll stand by you no matter which direction you go. I'll call the FBI myself if you want him arrested. I want whatever you want, Garnet."

She smoothed the fur around the bear's button eyes. "I'm already beginning to think more rationally. Sophie's grown more than I'd pictured," she said sadly. "I may be the woman in her bedside photo, but in her mind I'm pretty much a stranger. She won't come with me happily, will she? There'll be tantrums and tears."

"I doubt the FBI would give you instant custody, Garnet. There are rules and regulations they have to follow. They'll send a couple of agents to take Dale into custody, and another to take your statement. And since the kidnapping occurred in Alaska, they'll need time to verify your claim and get an update from the Anchorage police."

"What happens to Sophie? She stays with Dale's wife?"

Julian shook his head. "Social services will come for her. She'll be made a temporary ward of the court and placed in foster care until your case is sorted out."

"How awful for her. She'd be so frightened. How can they do that to a little girl?"

"Garnet, they do it to protect her. That's a good law—always do what's safest for the kids. It shouldn't take long for them to clear you, to prove you're a fit mom."

"My head is pounding. Having her life disrupted will confuse Sophie terribly. To be taken from all that's familiar could scar her for life."

Not knowing what else to do, Julian shrugged. "Kids are notably resilient. They also have an enormous capacity for love. You wouldn't believe how they can love moms and dads who aren't anywhere as normal as you or your ex."

"I'm ready to go back now," Garnet announced. "I'm ready to talk. To negotiate. I want a guarantee that Dale won't disappear with her the minute we leave here tonight."

"I'll have my folks come get you. And I'll ask one of my brothers to come trade his car for my motor-cycle. I'll stake out the house all night myself to make certain Dale doesn't hightail it again. Do you think he might?"

"Right now I'm taking it one step at a time."

The conversation at the picnic table stopped cold the minute Julian and Garnet reentered the backyard.

Sophie Patton caught sight of the stuffed toy Garnet clutched. She scrambled off the bench. "Bear-bear," she shouted. "Daddy, it's Bear-bear." She ran up to Garnet, and before Garnet could kneel to the child's level, Sophie snatched the toy and dashed straight back to her father. She hopped on his lap and hugged the bear to her. Her eyes were dark pools of distrust.

Garnet wilted. Julian had to grasp her elbow and propel her to the chairs at the end of the long table.

Liza excused herself from her family. "I put your burgers in the warming tray of the barbecue," she said. "Boys, pass them buns and fixings while I go get the meat."

"Please, nothing for me. Oh, but Julian, are you hungry?" Garnet blinked at him, plainly not wanting to put words in his mouth.

Liza hovered uncertainly. "Well, the kids had big appetites. They've already scarfed down their food. Why don't you three go play on the swings? Give us adults a few minutes alone to talk."

"What about the cake?" Toby asked, rubbing his belly.

"Yeah, Mom," Gavin added, not concealing his hostility toward the interlopers. "Tonight was supposed to be a family celebration because you and Lee got married yesterday. Uh, you and *Dale,* I mean."

Liza turned red and twisted the modest diamond ring around on her finger. "Hush, Gavin. I explained a minute ago."

The boy flung himself away from the table. He glared at Julian as if he was totally responsible for the upsetting situation. "C'mon, Toby and Leah… uh, Sophie. Shoot, maybe I'll call you Sophie Leah. Let's go swing and let Mom and Dad talk to these people."

Garnet didn't realize how tightly she held Julian's right arm until Liza brought his hamburger and he awkwardly attempted to put ketchup and mustard on the bun with his other hand.

Dale didn't miss their entwined arms. "You two an item?"

"Oh, uh…" Garnet quickly released her hold, freeing Julian.

"Sort of," he answered for both of them. "That's not what we are here to talk about," he said pointedly as he put his burger together.

Liza and Dale sat at one end of the table and Julian and Garnet at the other. With the children gone, the tension mounted.

Planting his elbows on the wood tabletop, Dale laced his work-worn fingers together. A faint tremor betrayed his nervousness. "I did a really bad thing, Garnet. I guess I snapped when it hit me that I'd only get an hour a week with Sophie, and it had to be supervised by a social worker. You probably don't give a damn, but at the time I was so pissed about how your friends stood before the judge and assassinated me...my character. I swear they never saw me even close to falling-down drunk. The closest I ever came to being buzzed in public was the day we buried Liza's husband, Jim. He and I worked on the pipeline together and got laid off at the same time. Jim found a job with a logging outfit. The day he was killed, he phoned to say a guy had quit and he thought I could get the job. I was happy, thinking how pleased you'd be. Then he had the accident. Oh, hell, none of that matters now. You have every right to have me arrested."

A painful cry escaped Liza's lips and she leaned her head on his shoulder. "She's your daughter, too, Dale. You took Leah because you love her. Sophie, I mean." She turned her weepy blue eyes to Garnet. "I don't know what happened between you two. I never asked. I know Dale is a good man and a devoted father who would never hurt this little girl. He's...not like that."

"It's okay, honey," Dale crooned softly in her hair. "We both knew jail time was a possibility."

Julian swallowed a bite of his hamburger.

"Maybe you'd like to have your lawyer meet Garnet. You say he's in Atlanta?"

"Would you wait that long before phoning the feds?" Dale seemed heartened by the possibility.

Garnet sat as if she'd turned to stone, her eyes rarely leaving the children on the play set. She especially watched Sophie, who hadn't let go of Bearbear even to swing.

Julian leaned close to draw her into the conversation. "Even with traffic he might make it here in forty minutes. Garnet, what do you say?" Glancing at Dale again, he added, "She's worried that you'll hit the road the minute her back is turned." Julian put down his burger and took Garnet's cold hand. "I'll grant you, the lawyer is on Dale's payroll, but he'll also be a trained negotiator," he murmured near her ear.

"All right. Call him. I doubt you have any idea of the sleepless nights I've had because of you, Dale, or the buckets of tears I've cried. I was already distraught over failing at marriage. When you took Sophie and with no word, well, only the death of a loved one can compare. I should hate you. Weeks ago I would've said I did." Garnet turned her face up to Julian's. "Then Julian showed up, bringing the only lead I'd had for ages. Helping me, he's also made me see that this isn't about me or you, Dale. It's about Sophie and what's best for her. It's always been about that, but at our hearing in Anchorage, I was too focused on my failures to understand how one-sided the judge's decree was."

"It's good that you two are finally talking about what happened," Liza said. "Shall I go inside and phone Harper Knight? I'll put on some coffee to have with the cake."

Dale and Garnet barely inclined their heads, but Liza took that as a yes and bounded off, calling the children to come in for milk and cake.

Again Garnet's gaze followed her child. A girl running and laughing delightedly into the house behind the two boys. Her stepbrothers.

The screen door banged on their heels and Garnet snapped to attention. Then her chin dropped and her eyelashes masked the pain in her eyes. "We don't need your lawyer, Dale. Sophie laughs like she's happy. And she has siblings. I hated being an only child. I thought she'd be living like a recluse, but that's not the case." Garnet lifted her head, her eyes still swimming in tears. "I love her too much to totally disrupt her life. We need to figure out what to do. To do what's best for Sophie."

Julian felt her anguish. "You're an amazing woman, Garnet," he said, sliding an arm around her, his fingers clasping her shoulder. "But you can't go back to Anchorage to break down quietly by yourself. You should be raising Sophie together. You don't love each other anymore, but you both deserve to watch her grow, cheer her accomplishments and listen when she has failures. You're a good teacher, Garnet. There must be schools around here that could use you."

"Yes. I could move here. Dale and I could share custody."

"Thank you, Garnet. You humble me with your generosity," Dale said with tremendous emotion from the other end of the table. "I swear all I ever wanted was an equal share in Sophie's life. I know you and I had our problems. They were as much my fault as yours. But we did something great when we had Sophie. Liza's been homeschooling her, and she's smart as a whip. She takes after you that way."

Garnet held up a shaking hand. "Don't say more. I can't handle hearing what I've missed. I bought books to read to her, Dale. You know she and I shared story time every night. How could you take her away like that? I don't understand."

Dale's face fell and he clasped his hands together. "The hell of it is, I don't understand, either. After the ruling, I went back to my apartment and it was like a dam broke. I'd just planned to take her out for lunch, but when I heard the sirens and saw the cop cars swooping down on the school, I knew I had to run or I'd go to jail and never see her again. My biker friends helped me leave Alaska. But I don't think like a criminal. I went to my brother's in Washington. But I had to move on without stopping. There were cops all over his farm. Then I thought of Liza. Falling in love with her was nothing I anticipated. It probably won't make any difference to you, but she's made me a better man."

Garnet rubbed her temples vigorously. "I have to go. I think I'm going to be sick." She rose shakily and Julian jumped up to assist her.

The screen opened and Liza came out carrying coffee cups and a cake with a wedge cut out. "The kids asked to watch the Disney Channel and eat their cake in the rec room. Uh…Mr. Knight has a family wedding tonight. He asked if we could all meet here tomorrow morning at ten." She set the tray down and glanced around hopefully.

"Yes, fine," Garnet said, preparing to flee. "Dale, I want your word Sophie will be here when we return in the morning."

Bracing himself on the table, Dale rose. "Contrary to what you think, Garnet, life on the run isn't anything I enjoy. Losing weight helped disguise me, but I developed ulcers from always looking over my shoulder. I couldn't even call my parents to see how they were. I'll be here tomorrow, and the day after and the year after that if you don't turn me in. I hope you believe that."

Garnet didn't respond. She had one hand cupped over her mouth and the other arm wrapped around her waist. Julian couldn't remember ever seeing anyone as close to the breaking point as Garnet. "Be here tomorrow or you'll live to regret it," he snapped at Dale. Not wasting another moment, Julian hustled Garnet out. At the bike, he handed Garnet her helmet, and over her shoulder he noticed the three children, their noses pressed against the front window.

"Sophie's watching," he murmured. "Wave to her, Garnet. It's time to build bridges with her, sweetheart."

Turning around, Garnet tentatively raised her hand. The youngest boy waved. Then Sophie smiled and waved with her bear.

CHAPTER TEN

THEY WERE ONLY twelve miles from the Cavenaugh house. "Hang on," Julian said. "We'll be at my parents' in no time." In Missouri, Garnet had said she was up for this, but Julian knew today had been harder than she anticipated.

Dusk gave way to full darkness not long before Julian parked his bike next to his parents' garage. Garnet was as fragile as a feather hanging on to his waist. She climbed woodenly off the seat and fumbled in her attempt to unfasten her helmet.

"You need a hot bath and a soft bed," Julian said, taking off her helmet and guiding her to the front door.

Garnet shook her hair out of her eyes. "I need one of your mom's energy drinks. I want to be more myself at tomorrow's meeting." She stopped him on the top step. "Do you think I need a lawyer? I've been thinking on the ride here, what you said about the attorney being on Dale's payroll. Will that give Dale an unfair advantage?"

"Sweetheart, I've seen Harper Knight in court. He's brilliant, and, to the best of my knowledge, honest. I predict all three of them are going to be tripping over themselves to make sure you're happy. Garnet, you're in control now. Don't you see what a truly magnanimous gesture you made tonight?"

"It's what you suggested I do…for Sophie's sake."

He passed a hand over his whisker-dark jaw. "And it's a sound theory. I can't tell you how many cases I've witnessed where some compromise for the sake of the kids would've been ideal. You're the first person I've seen put the idea into action."

"What? How do you know it's the best practice then?"

"You saw her, sweetheart. It *is* the right thing for your daughter. In my eyes, that makes you a hero."

"I don't feel heroic."

The front door swung open. Beth stepped outside and greeted Garnet with a hug while Sam waited in the doorway. "We heard Julian's bike, and then voices out here for too long. What happened? Garnet, we kept expecting you to phone to have us come after you and Sophie."

"Mom, give Garnet a break. She's had a rough time of it. But she handled everything brilliantly."

The Cavenaughs had a fire blazing in the living room. Sam ushered the tired couple to seats near the hearth.

Garnet hadn't really paid attention to this particular room before. The woodwork was white, the walls painted a warm yellow. Matching chintz sofas were arranged in a cozy *U* in front of the fire. The effect was so homey it made her heartache more profound.

"We were having amaretto coffee," Beth said. "It'll just take a minute to fix two more."

"None for me, thank you." Garnet dropped down on a couch, and stretched out her hands to warm them by the fire.

"Garnet's nerves are frayed as you might imagine. Before you came out, Mom, she was just saying she needed one of your energy shakes."

"Of course! And you, Julian? What can I get you?"

"I could use a beer. But I'll get it." He followed his mother into the kitchen and rummaged in the fridge until he found a beer to his liking. He smiled his thanks and left Beth tossing fruit and protein powder into the blender. He veered off into his dad's den and called a trustworthy private investigator he knew. Maybe Dale Patton was telling the truth about being tired of running. Then again, maybe he wasn't.

"Doug? Julian Cavenaugh here. Are you free for a stakeout tonight? Good. It's personal, not for the department." He gave the P.I. Dale's address. "Make sure the occupants stay put. If they don't call my cell. Thanks. I'll come around next week to settle the bill."

Back in the living room, Julian sat and listened to Garnet catching his dad up on the events of the day.

Sam sipped his Amaretto-laced coffee. Garnet's raspy voice gave out when she started describing why she'd left Sophie with Dale and his new wife. Sam nodded.

"You made a difficult choice."

"What choice was that?" Beth asked, coming into the room and setting a tall, frosty glass on the coffee table in front of Garnet. "I hope you like orange-cranberry."

Julian pressed the drink into Garnet's hands. "Drink," he insisted. "I'll give my mom the recap."

Beth's reaction was practical, not philosophical. "The child can only get reacquainted with you if she's actually *with* you." Leaning over, she patted

Garnet's knee. "As we say in tennis, dear, we need to get the ball back in your court."

Julian paused with the beer at his lips, and Garnet did the same with her glass. "What have you got in mind?" Sam asked.

"If I were you, I'd want that meeting tomorrow on my turf. Ten is a perfect time for brunch. We'll gather the Cavenaugh clan and make it a family event. You say Dale has the upper hand because he's given Sophie brothers. Julian's sister, Celeste, has twins. Girls a few months older than Sophie. Our other sons, Tag and Josh, have one boy each, and Raine, Tag's wife, is pregnant. Isn't the better plan to invite Dale and his lawyer here?"

No one answered, so Beth continued. "You know what I'm saying. What's gotten into you all? I'll wager that by tomorrow afternoon Sophie will be begging her dad for a sleepover here with Jocelyn and Kaylee."

Sam grinned. "I see where you're going with this. You, Garnet and the three girls will make sugar cookies and bond."

"And," Beth said with a smug grin, "Garnet can handle story time before bed. Dear, you told me you always read a bedtime story to Sophie. Her subconscious will surely remember the sound of her mother's voice."

Garnet finally seemed to relax. "Beth, you're so kind. This whole trip I've imagined Sophie seeing me and leaping into my arms. At the same time, a nagging little voice warned to expect the opposite. Still, I was crushed when she grabbed her bear and ran straight to Dale, cuddling on his lap instead of mine."

"Most girls Sophie's age are bashful," Beth said. "Add to that the precautions they must have taken to keep her from being seen. Sam, you and Julian both saw how protective they were. That alone would make her nervous around new people."

"You're right, Mom. You're also right about Garnet standing up for herself. I should have thought of it, but…seeing her so upset rattled me." His eyes sought Garnet's, and the love he wanted to convey remained unspoken.

Beth and Sam exchanged knowing smiles. "Naturally it's unsettling when someone you care about goes through an ordeal," Beth soothed. "So, are we agreed? We have a plan for tomorrow? If so, we'll start making calls. I was wondering, though, have either of you thought about what you want to do next?"

Garnet set her empty glass on the table, and stared bewildered at Beth.

Julian crushed his empty beer can between his hands. He thought he knew what his mom was really asking. "You mean like when I'm due back at work in Atlanta? The chief gave me an extra two weeks' leave."

Sam cleared his throat. "Your mom is probably asking when Garnet plans on going back to her life in Alaska."

"She's off work for the summer. Can't she stay here until she can make some clearheaded decisions?" Julian demanded a tad hotly. "The best thing for Sophie would be to have both of her parents nearby. I suggested Garnet see what teaching jobs are open in Wimberly or Mosswood, or somewhere around here."

"Like Atlanta," his mom slid in easily.

Julian jerked involuntarily. He twisted the crushed can in half. "Okay, Mom. Since you're meddling, that would be my preference, yes. But…" He expelled a breath and stood. "That's not practical for Sophie. She'll be starting first grade in the fall, and Garnet's not going to be content to see her only during school breaks. It makes sense for her and Dale to live in the same school district."

"If I'm inconveniencing you by staying here," Garnet said, "I'm sure I can find an inexpensive room or apartment to rent."

"Heavens, that's not what I was getting at," Beth stressed, scowling at her son. "Sam and I want you to stay all summer, Garnet. Or longer."

Remaining stubbornly silent on the subject of his relationship with Garnet, because he wasn't at all sure where they stood, Julian headed for the kitchen with his mangled can. "I'll call Josh and Tag. Mom, you invite Celeste. Oh, Garnet, here's Dale's phone number." Turning back briefly, Julian tore the page out of his notebook and handed it to her. "Tell them to call their lawyer and say you'd rather meet on neutral territory. Make sure they know to bring the kids and that Mom is serving brunch."

"All right. Is something going on? Julian, you sound angry."

Beth twirled a dainty hand. "He's not angry with you, Garnet. He's annoyed with me for meddling."

Garnet frowned. "I thought we all agreed your idea to meet here was a good one."

"That idea, yes," Julian said from the doorway.

Sam got to his feet. "Beth is prying into Julian's private life, and while that's normal, it doesn't set well with him. Say…before you get busy with other things, son, there's something I've been meaning to bring up. Mosswood's police chief, J. C. Bitterman, announced he's retiring in September. Rumor has it that our city council wants to replace him with someone younger. It crossed my mind that a hometown boy might have an advantage in an interview."

Julian had started to walk on, but slowed his steps and waited for his father to catch up. "So, Pop, what credentials do you think they're looking for?"

Sam settled a hand on his son's shoulder and the men walked out of the room, leaving Beth and Garnet in front of the crackling fire.

"Doesn't that beat all. Meddling from his father is okay, but not from me," Beth said with a hint of exasperation.

"Julian has been so good to me. Well, you all have," Garnet added quickly. "I'd hate to think I'm causing a family disagreement."

"Cavenaugh family squabbles are legendary. Don't let it bother you, Garnet. You have more than enough on your plate as it is." Beth linked her arm with Garnet's. "Let's go upstairs to my study. I'll phone Celeste, then introduce you to the family through the albums. Maybe it'll help prepare you for tomorrow. We tend to bicker. It's friendly, and doesn't mean anything. We share a much deeper love that binds us together."

"I can certainly see the love between you, Sam and Julian. When I try to compare what I see in this house with my own family, I can't. My parents used the word *duty* a lot. Not that I was mistreated. I had food, clothes and a roof over my head. My education was hugely important. But the love was missing. You know, Beth, I'm afraid my upbringing affected my marriage. Dale never looked at me the way I saw him looking at Liza today. I wasn't the best wife. Maybe I don't know how to be one. I was, however, an excellent mother. The moment I held Sophie in my arms, I was overcome with emotion. I didn't recognize it then as love. I just remember thinking that I'd go to the ends of the earth to make sure my daughter never felt…insignificant. If you'd heard how she laughed with Liza's boys today… She's happy there. I felt so jealous. What does that say about me, Beth?"

"Garnet, you grew up emotionally starved. Dale obviously didn't see it. But I don't buy for a minute that you can't be as good a wife as Liza, or me, or anyone."

As they entered the study, Beth went on. "I hope you aren't suggesting that Sophie would be better off living full-time with Dale. She doesn't have amnesia. She'll remember you feeding and bathing her, and the million other little things mothers do for their children. Right now you're in shock. After a good night's sleep you'll recall all the times you and Sophie laughed together."

"We did. We did. Oh, Beth, thank you for reminding me of that. Hand me the phone, please. I'm going to call Dale and tell him about the change in plans. I'll point out how lucky he is that I'm even willing to consider not pressing charges. Then, if you don't mind, after we look at your family albums, may I borrow the local phone book? I'd like to make a list of local schools where I can send a résumé. Do you think Julian will lend me his laptop?" She hesitated.

"If I read Julian correctly, Garnet, he'll give you his laptop and anything else that will help you. Can't you tell how much he cares about you? There is such love on his face when he looks at you."

Garnet blushed. "You raised a compassionate son. But he doesn't really know me, Beth. He's been very kind and supportive, and I'm so glad I had him with me today. I couldn't have done this alone. I care about him a great deal, but..." She bent her head and fought the heat spilling into her cheeks. "I'm just one of his cases."

"I think I can say with confidence that what he feels toward you goes far deeper than that."

"What if I don't deserve him? The end of a marriage is never one-sided. At the time Dale and I decided to divorce it was easy for me to place all of the blame on him. My friends tried to boost my ego. And when he stole Sophie, I was absolved of any fault. Today I saw him through the eyes of people who don't think I walk on water. Sophie, for one. And kids are honest judges of character."

"So is Julian. Call Dale, Garnet. And try not to be so hard on yourself. We all need to work at making relationships work. The best thing about humans is we have the power to change ourselves."

Talk fell off. Garnet made her call to Dale, and Beth phoned her daughter. Then together they sat and looked at Cavenaugh family albums and laughed over some of Julian's school pictures until Beth noticed Garnet's eyes drooping. "We can look at the remaining pictures another day. You're exhausted. Go get some rest and tomorrow will be better."

"I wanted to borrow your phone book. And a pad and pen, if I may."

"Should you dive into that project tonight? Oh, listen to me talking to you like one of my kids."

Garnet smiled. "The fact that you do means more to me than you'll ever know."

Beth rose, found the directory and other items for Garnet. "Then you won't mind if I pray that a teaching job will open up, and that our city council will be moved to hire Julian as Mosswood's police chief?"

Garnet chewed her lip for a moment. "I probably should mind, but strangely enough, I don't."

Beth waited until Garnet had entered her bedroom and closed the door before she picked up the Cavenaugh album with its blank pages waiting for her oldest son's wedding and family photos.

Sam and Julian appeared in the doorway. "I suppose I shouldn't ask why you're looking so pleased with yourself," Julian said, eyeing his mother suspiciously.

"I'm always happy when I know the family is going to be together for a weekend brunch. We are, aren't we?" she asked as she slid the album back in its jacket. "Josh and Tag said they'll come?"

"When have we ever asked them to drop all plans

and show up here on a moment's notice?" Sam asked. "They'll probably speculate that we're going to announce a decision to move to a retirement village and sell Julian the house."

"All in good time." Beth brushed past them, patting both on their cheeks. "Don't wait up for me, Sam. I have a menu to plan."

"She's up to something," Julian said once his mother had disappeared down the stairs.

"You'll go crazy trying to figure it out."

Saying good-night to his father, Julian passed Garnet's door and hesitated. He should have asked his mom how long ago Garnet had gone to bed. He was too keyed up to sleep, and kept thinking about the possibility of her finding a local teaching job and his applying for the chief's job in Mosswood. A few months ago, the idea of settling down with one special woman would have been foreign. Now he hated the thought of going back to Atlanta without her.

Retracing his steps, Julian tapped on her door.

She called a muffled, "Come in."

He entered and found Garnet seated cross-legged in the middle of her bed. She had on a stretched-out nightshirt. One finger marked her place in the phone book, and she had a pencil between her teeth. She looked so delectable, Julian couldn't help tugging away the pencil and kissing her.

"What was that for?" she asked, her heart galloping even as he lifted his mouth.

"Nothing special. What are you doing?"

"Making a list of schools in the vicinity. I'll need a job before I can look for housing. Are you off to bed?"

"Not yet. Garnet, my mom meant it when she said you could stay here as long as you like."

"I know. And that's very sweet of her. But I'll want to live in Sophie's school district."

"In Wimberly, you mean? How about Mosswood?" Julian moved Garnet's paper and the phone book to give him room to join her on the bed.

"Mosswood is beautiful. Wimberly is the older of the two communities, right? And is probably more affordable. I'll lose my tenure starting over in a new district. Which means my salary will be lower, so I'll have to watch my pennies. I think I can move everything I need in my car. I do owe you for a round-trip plane ticket, and that's good. There are people who will want to hear my news. People I need to hug goodbye. Anna, John, Hazel and Jenny to name a few."

"You'll need to notify the Anchorage police and the FBI that you've decided to withdraw your kidnapping complaint against Dale. His lawyer can draw up an affidavit for you to sign, providing you still feel the same way tomorrow."

"I will. I'm determined to be part of Sophie's life again, yet cause her the least disruption."

Julian took Garnet's hands in his and played with her slender fingers. "Keep in mind you don't have to make all the concessions."

"What are you talking about? You persuaded me to forgive Dale. Hard as that is, I agree it's what's best for Sophie. Why are you unhappy, Julian?"

"I'm not. Well, okay, I am. Dale's the one who broke the law. He should get down on his knees and thank you for not having him arrested. Giving him equal custody is like rewarding him. You shouldn't have to rearrange your life around what he wants. You set the limits here. Let Dale be the one to conform."

"I just thought since he and Liza bought a house, and I'm the one in limbo…" She looked at Julian and saw that his eyes were dark and troubled. "I'm still missing something. Tell me. I owe you so much—I want to make you happy."

He clasped her shoulders and pulled her close. "I

talked to Pop tonight about buying this house. When he retires in a few months, they plan to downsize. I've decided to apply for the police chief position in Mosswood. Even if I don't get that I can do private security. Last Christmas, Tag asked me to move home and take over as head security officer at the resort hotel that he manages just south of here. If I seem unhappy, Garnet, it's because I've been figuring you'd be a part of any changes I make in my life. Am I reading us wrong?"

She sat up, lifted a hand and traced the serious lines bracketing his mouth. "Live here, in this house? With you?" she asked breathlessly.

"Sophie, too, fifty percent of the time. And maybe down the line give her a half brother or sister. Before I went to Anchorage, I would've said I'd always be single. I didn't figure on meeting you and falling in love."

"I didn't imagine I'd meet anyone like you, either…not ever," she murmured, stretching to kiss him.

Warmth spread through his chest and left his bones weak as he pressed her down into the softness of the pillows. When she opened his shirt and found his skin, Julian remembered how long he'd been starved for love. Starved and lonely. He inched up her worn nightshirt. "I want to buy you something skimpy in satin."

"There are rules that come with having a nosy, five-year-old in the house. Moms are covered neck-to-ankle in flannel. And dads wear at least the bottom half of pj's or sweats."

Julian groaned even as he kicked off his boots and Garnet stripped him of his jeans. "Georgia is too hot for flannel. I'll install a lock on the bedroom door."

At that comment, Garnet lifted her head. "Julian, where's your mom? What if she wants to tell me something about tomorrow and comes in?"

He straddled her, urging her to lie flat, and barely managed to say, "A true Southern lady would never enter a guest's bedroom without knocking first."

Garnet opened her mouth to ask another question, but Julian covered her mouth with his. It was a long time later before he left her mouth unattended, or for that matter, the rest of her body. By then, Garnet's mind was blank and she had no idea what she'd planned to ask.

BANGING DOORS and voices in the hall woke Garnet. She was alone in bed and light streamed in through curtains she'd forgotten to close the night before. Julian was gone, but the memories lingered. Sometime in the night he'd asked her to be his wife. She was touched by it, and showed him how much. By the same token, she'd asked for some time to get reacquainted with her daughter, and to get her own life squared away before they committed themselves to marriage.

He'd been disappointed, she thought as she headed for the shower. Until she'd explained that she just needed to get through this nerve-racking day. Julian said he understood. From the tender way he'd kissed her after that, and made love to her, she knew he did.

They met on the stairs. "Good morning, sleepyhead," he said, then stole a kiss that sent heat to Garnet's cheeks.

"You should've set the alarm when you left," she whispered.

"Um, there's something I have to tell you. Our secret's out. I bumped into Mom coming upstairs from the kitchen as I sneaked out of your room."

"You didn't."

"Yep. And she's already blabbed to Tag, Raine, Josh, Dawn and Pop. Miles, Celeste and the twins just pulled in. Mom was on her way out to meet them, so I came up to warn you. Sorry, I don't know what I could've done to silence her short of threatening to break her kneecaps." He grinned. "I'm not sure that would've worked, either. Don't look so distressed. Everyone will be happy for us," he said. "I told them it will be fall before we even think about planning a wedding."

"That's good."

"Yeah, but don't be surprised if Taggert says we need to get a date for the reception on the catering book at his resort. Mom will bug you about arranging for the church. Celeste's girls will bug you to let them be flower girls. They were recently in a wedding for one of my sister's friends. According to Mom, they're instant experts. And flower-girl dresses are the coolest ever."

MEETING THE NOISY Cavenaugh clan was a dizzying experience. However, Garnet's warm acceptance into the family was an experience she'd often dreamed about.

Dale, Liza and family were ten minutes late, which had Garnet pacing in front of the window. "I was imagining he'd skipped out again," she said, clinging to Julian as they watched Liza's boys climb out of the backseats of a minivan.

"Sweetheart, no. While you were chatting with Pop last night, I arranged for a P.I., an ex-cop who retired from our department, to stake out Dale's house."

"You did that for me? If I didn't already love you, that would do it. Oh, look. Sophie brought her bear. I knew he was important to her."

Julian lightly massaged Garnet's neck. "Give her time. She'll start remembering you as more than the mommy in the photograph."

"I hope so. I don't see their lawyer."

Harper Knight arrived before Dale and family reached the front door.

Always gracious hosts, Beth and Sam made short work of introductions. Beth had set up a buffet brunch in the large, comfortable family room to put the newcomers at ease. "We'll eat first and get better acquainted," Beth said, "then Tag, Josh and Miles can take the kids out in the backyard to play while Raine, Dawn, Celeste and I clean up. The rest of you and Mr. Knight can get down to business."

It seemed to be a good plan, and Sam passed around sturdy paper plates so that the crowd could get straight to filling them.

Garnet helped herself, but she was too jumpy to eat. Instead, she feasted her eyes on Sophie. The girl gravitated to Celeste's twins as Beth had predicted. But when midway through the meal the twins hopped up to ask their grandmother for more milk, Sophie paused next to Garnet. "I remember you bought me a furry pink jacket. A boy named Jason pushed me down at school and got mud all over the front. I cried and cried. You said you could wash the dirt out. And you did. I still have the jacket, but it doesn't fit me too good anymore."

"I'm sure it doesn't, Sophie, er…would you rather I call you Leah?" Garnet asked, feeling her way.

"I kinda remember that used to be my name. Last night, Daddy said my real name is Sophie Leah. I think I like Sophie. It sounds like a big girl's name."

"You have grown a lot taller since I last saw you. But I expect your pink jacket would be too warm in Georgia, anyway."

"That's what Liza said. Daddy asked her to take it apart and make me a pillow for my bed, 'cause I loved it so much."

Garnet's breath caught. She'd spent too much on the jacket and Dale had complained. She glanced at him now, and saw his indulgent smile. "That was a nice thing for Liza to do."

"Uh-huh. I like her." Sophie spun around on one foot, then on the other. She spotted the twins coming back and she started to follow them, but turned back and said, "I like you, too."

Garnet felt her throat close, but managed to say, "And I li—love you."

"Last night, Daddy said you're my real mommy. He said I'm lucky to have two mommies. Did you used to cover me up with a princess quilt, and read me princess stories before I went to sleep?"

"Yes, oh, yes, I did."

"Uh-huh. You know what? I'm glad you moved to Georgia." Turning, Sophie skipped off to join Kaylee and Jocelyn.

Julian, who'd watched and listened to that exchange play out from a distance, caught Garnet's eye and flashed her a discreet thumbs-up.

Beaming, Garnet blotted her tears, and returned to the buffet to get a second helping of pecan blintzes. "I guess I'm hungry after all," she murmured to Julian as he handed her a cup of coffee.

Sophie's few memories were the encouragement Garnet had needed to take control of the meeting. The case was no longer about kidnapping, but about hammering out an equitable, if belated, custody agreement.

"Garnet, why can't you move to Wimberly?" Dale said at one point in the negotiations. "I've just bought a home three blocks from a good school. We need Sophie at the grade school next door to Gavin's middle school. That way, he can pick up Toby and Sophie and walk them home. Liza needs a year of in-hospital training to complete her nursing degree. She won't always be able to leave on the dot of three o'clock, either."

"Frankly, that's your problem," Garnet said. "I'm going to live in Mosswood. Right here, in fact. Julian is buying this house from his parents. He and I are discussing having a fall wedding." She reached back and grasped Julian's hand. He hadn't joined the three sitting around the table with the attorney, but he was a solid presence behind Garnet's chair.

Julian's heart tripped ecstatically hearing the easy way she announced the news to everyone within hearing range, including his mother, his sister and sisters-in-law.

Dale sat up straighter. "I didn't know. But I don't

see how that changes anything. Sophie has to attend a school with and near the boys. They're her brothers."

"Stepbrothers," Garnet shot back. "If we decide she'll be with you part of each school year, you or Liza can drop Sophie off at the school at the end of this cul-de-sac. Julian or I will see that she gets to your home on the appropriate days or weekends. That's another thing. I want a rotating schedule for summers and holidays. We aren't going to say one or the other of us always gets her on the Fourth of July or Christmas."

"What you're proposing makes any kind of routine difficult," Dale complained.

Harper Knight cleared his throat. "Dale, you aren't in any position to make demands. When you invited me to this meeting, I came fully prepared to bargain for thirty years instead of life. Compared to that, driving Sophie twelve miles one way over the course of a few school years seems a small price to pay."

Liza gripped Dale's knee and his bluster fell away. "You're right, of course. Forgive me, Garnet. I let myself forget my situation for a moment."

The back door opened then and Sophie breezed in with the twins. "Daddy, Daddy," she exclaimed.

"Kaylee and Jocelyn get to stay here all night tonight. They're going to make sugar cookies and have popcorn and sleep in sleeping bags on the living-room floor. They invited me. Can I stay? Please?"

Garnet held her breath, waiting for Dale to refuse. He truly had done an about-face. "I don't see why not, Sophie. As long as it's all right with your mother."

"With Liza momma, or my real momma?" Sophie asked, darting excited eyes between the two women seated across the table from each other.

Again, Garnet took the lead. "Beginning today, Sophie, you're going to have to get an agreement between Liza, me and your father. And Julian, after we become part of his family."

"See, we told you so," Kaylee announced boldly. "We heard Mama tell Daddy that Uncle Julian's going to marry your mama, Sophie. Hooray, hooray! That means we'll all be cousins! And flower girls at the wedding, right, Auntie Garnet? May Jocelyn and me call you Auntie?"

"Auntie…yes, please, I like that," Garnet said, breaking into a smile. "But, Kaylee, since I'm a teacher, you should have said Jocelyn and *I*."

A collective chuckle went up from the various

adults. And when the boys and the men came in from the yard, they were informed of the new developments.

Harper Knight gathered his briefcase and prepared to leave. "Garnet, I'll prepare briefs for you to sign, dropping all charges against Dale. I must say you're a very generous person. I wish there were more like you."

Checking that Sam wasn't around, Knight added, "Someone in this group ought to nominate Mr. Cavenaugh for Georgia's citizen of the year. I think the committee accepts submissions through the end of June."

Knight stood, saying he would get the documents to them within a couple of weeks. "A judge has to sign off on the custody agreement," he said from the doorway. "We've done the hard work, I don't expect any problem."

After the lawyer had gone, Julian and his siblings—and Dale—conferred over whether they should send a joint letter to the nominations committee, or if it would be better to each write a separate letter.

Garnet volunteered to contribute, saying, "No matter how many you send, I'll add a heartfelt postscript to each. There probably aren't enough words to express my gratitude for what he did."

The discussion halted the minute Sam entered the room. Tag popped the cork on a bottle of champagne Julian had found in a cupboard, and they all toasted the man responsible for bringing about this happy reunion.

CHAPTER ELEVEN

SEPTEMBER WAS MILDLY cooler than from the sweaty ninety-degree weather they'd suffered throughout July and August. Mosswood evenings were balmy, which was why Beth and Taggert were attempting to talk Julian and Garnet into having their wedding reception on the twelfth-floor patio of Tag's hotel.

"The wedding is two weeks away," Julian said. "How do we know a rainstorm won't blow up from the gulf?"

"I checked the long-term forecast," Tag said. "No storms brewing in the Caribbean. I can promise hotel staff won't set tables up until the morning of the reception. If it looks even remotely like rain we'll move everything into one of the banquet rooms. Come on, Julian, ease up. The ambiance is better on the patio and the combo we booked to play for the dance prefer it, too."

"Combo." Garnet rolled her eyes. "This wedding started off small and intimate."

Beth spoke soothingly as she'd done frequently during the planning stages of the wedding. "I know you didn't want a big to-do. You'll have the intimacy at the chapel, Garnet. But with Julian now the chief of police, the reception had to be bigger," she noted with a mother's pride. She glanced around, then lowered her voice. "It was your idea, Garnet, to combine the presentation of Samuel's citizen of the year award with your wedding reception. Don't get me wrong, I think it's a great decision. This way Sam won't have to wear a tux twice. He says his idea of retirement is never having to wear a tie again."

"You think Pop has any idea he's being honored?" Julian asked.

"Not unless someone let it slip around one of the grandkids."

Garnet looked worried until Julian said, "Naw, the kids are too distracted by their own events. First the girls got new dresses for the christening of Tag and Dawn's new baby boy. Then Mom took them all shopping for school clothes, which was a huge hit."

Celeste, who had stopped over to collect her twins, heard the last part of the exchange. "Julian's so right, Garnet. Since you mailed the invitations they've all been consumed with practicing their duties for your wedding and reception. I know if Sophie, Kaylee or Jocelyn overheard anything that didn't involve them getting frilly floor-length gowns, they tuned it out."

"That's your doing, Beth," Garnet scolded with a genuine smile. "You're teaching those girls to be shopoholics."

"I'm making them proper Southern belles, one and all," Beth claimed, batting her eyelashes in exaggerated fashion.

Her sons, Celeste and Garnet laughed.

Tag got up to leave. "When you two lovebirds decide where you want the reception, call me. But you'd better be quick. The weather's so nice we've had a lot of interest in the patio. I've placed it on hold for you, but executive privilege only lasts so long. I'll have to release it soon."

"Book the patio," Garnet said, turning to Julian for confirmation. As if he would refuse her anything. Especially after she'd agreed to let him and his brothers fly to Anchorage in her stead and clear out her apartment. They'd driven her car and a trailer filled with her belongings back to Georgia, but not before Larry Adams had arranged for them to go deep-sea fishing. The three hadn't stopped bragging about the size of the salmon they'd caught. They'd donated their three fish to John Carlyle for another feast in Garnet's old apartment complex.

Garnet had stayed in Georgia to focus on job interviews, which turned out to be a good thing. Mosswood High School had hired her just a week ago to teach English, the subject she loved most, and at a school halfway between the Cavenaugh house and Dale and Liza's home in Wimberly.

"Phew, I'm glad that's settled," Tag exclaimed, referring back to Garnet's decision about the patio as he sprinted for the door. "And stop worrying. Garnet's already had enough bad luck for a lifetime."

THE WEDDING, as Garnet and Julian had requested, was performed by Beth and Sam's pastor in the small chapel where Beth had taken Garnet to pray on her first day in Georgia. The ceremony took place in front of a small group of immediate family and close friends, including Julian's former partner from Atlanta and his family and Chief MacHale.

Julian surprised Garnet by secretly inviting Anna Winkleman, Hazel Webber and John Carlyle to come as her family, since her own parents had declined to make the trip.

Before the ceremony, Anna and Hazel fussed over Garnet, making sure she wore something old, new, borrowed and blue. She hugged them both repeatedly, and shed a tear when Mr. Carlyle escorted her down the aisle strewn with satin rose petals.

Garnet's best friend, Jenny Hoffman, flew in from Anchorage and arrived at the ceremony on the arm of Julian's buddy, Larry Adams, shocking everyone.

Jenny pulled Garnet aside right after the service and the pair squealed in delight. "You look so fabulous and relaxed, Garnet." Jenny's eyes were bright with tears of joy. "Listen, I need to apologize for any part I had in exaggerating Dale's drinking problems to the family court judge. I'd take it all back if I could."

"It's over and done with, Jenny. I was the one who requested sole custody. It all worked out in the end, and I've never been happier than I am right now. Hey there, you're looking quite content yourself. I trust everything's going well for you?"

"Perfect. When we get back to Anchorage I'm moving in with Larry. It's a big step for us both, but after you left, we realized that we're happiest together."

The two pressed their foreheads together. "We've both been through a lot. But we've emerged stronger for our journeys," Jenny said, stepping away to let others enter the receiving line.

WHEN GARNET and Julian reached the reception at the resort hotel in the woods, it was as if the entire state of Georgia had been invited.

"Don't leave me alone," she ordered her new husband, clutching Julian's strong arm. "I'm scared to death I'll forget the mayor or his wife's name, or some other city council bigwig. The night you proposed, I didn't realize I'd be marrying a dignitary."

Julian smothered a laugh as he nibbled her neck, something he'd made a habit of doing whenever he managed to get her alone over the busy last few months. "Tell me again," he whispered, "which woman from Mom's salon is the one who introduced you to that peach lotion? I want to be sure to thank her. Have I mentioned that you are the most beautiful woman here, and you smell good enough to eat?"

"Only about a million times. Julian, if I'm beautiful it's because of how happy you've made me. Not only did you find Sophie, but you've given both of us something precious—a lovely extended family. Considering how shy she was that first afternoon, my darling daughter has turned into a regular social butterfly."

"She's the spitting image of you," Julian said, letting his hand slide up and down Garnet's bare arm. "I predict our daughter will one day have some guy as crazy for her as I am for her mother. Uh, Garnet, we did agree, didn't we—no dating until she's sixteen? I can't take the added strain."

Garnet laid her head on his wide shoulder. "You wear stepfatherhood well, Chief. Have you noticed how impressed Sophie is by your uniform? She thinks you look very handsome. And so do I."

"Thanks. But there'll come a day when she changes her mind and thinks my job is a pain in the you-know-what."

"Ah, you mean when the first young man she gets a mad crush on learns her dad's the city's head cop, and you have the poor boy shaking in his shoes?"

They laughed quietly. Then Julian tugged his wife out on the dance floor to kick off the evening's celebration.

Even more than dancing herself, Garnet loved to

stand off to the side and watch Sophie flit between Julian and her real dad. Dale said he and Liza had been humbled and delighted to be invited to the reception.

Sophie's laugh as both her dads waltzed her across the floor tugged at Garnet's heart.

Ten o'clock rolled around and the state governor swooped in with his entourage of officials. The Cavenaugh family had all been waiting impatiently for this moment.

The entire family drifted up to the bandstand, except for Sam, who remained oblivious even after Josh signaled for a drumroll.

Gavin and Toby left their mother and stepdad's side. The boys couldn't have been prouder to have been asked to escort Sam to the stage.

"What's going on?" he asked, as the boys each took an arm and dragged him forward.

The governor stepped up to the microphone. "Samuel Cavenaugh, on behalf of the state of Georgia, and through the deeply emotional letters our citizen-of-the-year committee received from your family, I'm very pleased to present you with this plaque for a meritorious deed many would have thought too risky. Because you were selfless and willing to put your retirement on the line, a child and her mother have been reunited. If the world had more citizens like you, Sam, and more families like yours, we'd all be better off. So I thank you, and trust you and Mrs. Cavenaugh will find some way to enjoy the twenty-five-hundred-dollar check that comes with the plaque. Oh, I almost forgot," he said, as Sam seemed incapable of speech. "Here are the letters your children wrote. The money will be gone and the brass plate on the plaque tarnished in time. But the love in these letters, I know, will be your true reward for many years to come."

The governor placed the stack of letters in Sam's shaking hands as the patio erupted in thunderous applause.

Beth rose on her toes and kissed her husband's damp cheek. Julian and Garnet scooped Sophie up so she could give Sam a hug. In the background, the combo began to play a dreamy rendition of the state song, "Georgia On My Mind," as guests crowded around the truly stunned man.

Tag and Raine, Josh and Dawn and Julian and Garnet moved into a clear space and started dancing.

But there wasn't a dry eye on the patio for quite some time.

Especially not when Sam and Beth gathered their grandchildren, and amid laughter and tears, circle-danced all of them around the patio beneath the golden moon shining overhead.

Dear Reader,

The most asked question of an author is "where do your ideas come from?" The answer is as diverse as the stories themselves. For me it's usually a snippet I read about or overhear that nags me to write my own version, as it was in this case.

A few years ago a reader wrote to say she'd read one of my books. In the letter she mentioned truth being stranger than fiction. Her husband, she said, a postman, was instrumental in reconnecting a child pictured on one of the lost children cards he delivered with the child's mother. Off and on I found myself wondering how it had all worked out. But since I didn't know the "real" story, I made up how I'd like for such a reunion to turn out. I like happy endings, and I like good people. I took liberties with this story that probably aren't true to life. Especially as I have a friend in social work who says domestic abductions rarely end well. More often than not the child ends up hurt, because children love both mom and dad equally.

In this book I wanted to delve into the feelings and emotions of two parents involved in such a case.

And since it's fiction, I really wanted the best possible ending for my stolen child, Sophie Patton. I hope you like her story.

Roz Denny Fox

Readers can contact me at
P.O. Box 17480-101
Tucson, AZ 85731 or,
rdfox@worldnet.att.net

Turn the page for a sneak preview
of the first book in the new miniseries
DIAMONDS DOWN UNDER
from Silhouette Desire®,
VOWS & A VENGEFUL GROOM
by Bronwyn Jameson

Available January 2008

Silhouette Desire®
Always Powerful, Passionate and Provocative

Kimberley Blackstone didn't notice the waiting horde of media until it was too late. Flashbulbs exploded around her like a New Year's light show. She skidded to a halt, so abruptly her trailing suitcase all but overtook her.

This had to be a case of mistaken identity. Surely. Kimberley hadn't been on the paparazzi hit list for close to a decade, not since she'd estranged herself from her billionaire father and his headline-hungry diamond business.

But no, it was *her* name they called. *Her* face was the focus of a swarm of lenses that circled her like avid hornets. Her heart started to pound with fear-fueled adrenaline.

What did they want?

What was going on?

With a rising sense of bewilderment she scanned the crowd for a clue, and her gaze fastened on a tall, leonine figure forcing his way to the front. A tall, familiar figure. Her head came up in stunned recognition, and their gazes collided across the sea of heads before the cameras erupted with another barrage of flashes, this time right in her exposed face.

Blinded by the flashbulbs—and by the shock of that momentary eye-meet—Kimberley didn't realize his intent until he'd forged his way to her side, possibly by the sheer strength of his personality. She felt his arm wrap around her shoulder, pulling her into the protective shelter of his body, allowing her no time to object. No chance to lift her hands to ward him off.

In the space of a hastily drawn breath, she found herself plastered knee-to-nose against six feet two inches of hard-bodied male.

Ric Perrini.

Her lover for ten torrid weeks, her husband for ten tumultuous days.

Her ex for ten tranquil years.

After all this time, he should not have felt so familiar but, oh, dear, he did. She knew the scent of that body and its lean, muscular strength. She knew its heat and its slick power and every response it could draw from hers.

She also recognized the ease with which he'd taken control of the moment and the decisiveness of his deep voice when it rumbled close to her ear. "I have a car waiting outside. Is this your only luggage?"

Kimberley nodded. "I assume you will tell me," she said tightly, "what this welcome party is all about."

"Not while the welcome party is within earshot. No."

Barking a request for the cameramen to stand aside, Perrini took her hand and pulled her into step with his ground-eating stride. Kimberley let him, because he was right, damn his arrogant, Italian-suited hide. Despite the speed with which he whisked her across the airport terminal, she could almost feel the hot breath of the pursuing media on her back.

This was neither the time nor the place for explanations. Inside his car, however, she would get answers.

Now that the initial shock had been blown away—by the haste of their retreat, by the heat of her gathering indignation, by the rush of adrenaline fired by Perrini's presence and the looming verbal battle—her brain was starting to tick over. This had to be her father's doing. And if it was a Howard

Blackstone publicity ploy, then it had to be about Blackstone Diamonds, the company that ruled his life.

The knowledge made her chest tighten with a familiar ache of disillusionment.

She'd known her father would be flying in from Sydney for today's opening of the newest in his chain of exclusive, high-end jewelry boutiques. The opulent shopfront sat adjacent to the rival business where Kimberley worked. No coincidence, she thought bitterly, just as it was no coincidence that Ric Perrini was here in Auckland ushering her to his car.

Perrini was Howard Blackstone's right-hand man, second in command at Blackstone Diamonds, a legacy of his short-lived marriage to the boss's daughter. No doubt her father had sent him to fetch her; the question was *why?*

* * * * *